First Dates, Last Calls

Front Is Peace

First Dates, Last Calls

Short Fiction by Alexandra Erin

Erin

Cover art by Amanda Sharpe
http://www.amandasharpe.com

Deco Card font by P.D. Magnus
http://www.fontmonkey.com

"Every woman I know has been storing anger for years

in her body and it's starting to feel like bees are going

to pour out of all of our mouths at the same time."

– Erin Keane

Table of Contents

A Temple for Persephone

Her suit, slimline, sublime,
sleek, slick as black ice,
lines sharp and straight
like an icepick.

Dangerous, too.

Dark, her eyes,
and thick, her hair.
Tousled, tangled, tufted.
Sweet, her smile.

Dangerous, too.

Careless shake
of a cocktail shaker.
Practiced flick
of a practiced wrist.

Click, clack, clatter
goes the ice.
Out comes the drink,
so ice-cold
I can feel it,
I can see it.

"What do you need?"
the bartender asks,

dark eyes gleaming,
smile still dangerous,
more dangerous now.

She saw me watching.
She saw me looking.
She saw me.

"I don't want anything," I say.

I don't want anything I can say.

Dark eyes
flick down,
then up.

Her voice,
not quite a whisper,
not yet a purr.

"Everybody

wants

something,

my dear."

My dear mother warned me
about wolves in sharp suits,
and about a certain kind of woman
I should never mix myself up with.

She never considered
they might be
the same,
never considered how
they might mix me up
instead, how I might be
shaken and poured out,
carried away.

This is not my scene.

Holiday party in a cocktail lounge.
Midtown, downtown, somewhere.

Underground.

You probably haven't heard of it.

I hadn't.

Work function,
coworkers functioning
barely and loudly.
Not my scene, but—
I couldn't
get out of it
if I'd tried.

I'd tried.

I couldn't
get out of it,
so I came, I came,
I went, I went around,
worked the floor,
worked the crowd,
circled the room.

Kept it moving.
Kept it light.
Kept an eye out for danger,
an eye on the clock,
and one more eye
than I had
on the exit.

Looking for my chance,
looking for the moment,
the very first moment
I could safely bolt
to safety.

Eye on the prize, oh, you know,
I've heard that one before.

Oh, yes.

How do you think I got here?
The same way I get anywhere:
I let myself be swept along.
I let myself get
carried away.

I came.

"Are you sure
I can't get you
a little
something?"

Her suit is dangerous,
her voice is low.
Her eyes are dark,
her eyes are kind.

In a room full of hunger,
every kind of appetite,
her eyes are kind
and a little
sad.

I'm not ready for that.
Braced for every kind of danger,
I wasn't ready for that.

I'd passed
on the cheese trays,
the smoked salmon,
the stuffed mushrooms,
the rings of shrimp,
the trays of champagne.

Never a picky eater, I've just
never trusted anything
that sat out in the open,
rarely ate anything
I hadn't seen prepared,
made for myself.

Old habits,
almost superstitions.

I so rarely drink,
never take drinks
proffered by a stranger.

It's different when it's the bartender,
I tell myself. It's different.
She's different.

Something's different.

Something.

Maybe.

"Maybe something," I agree.
"Maybe a little.
Maybe something...
a little bit like a
Shirley Temple?"

The bartender's eyes flick
down, and then up.

"Sure," she says.
"A little something
like a Shirley Temple.
Like a Temple, how?
What do you seek,
the sweetness
or the safety?"

I think;
I don't think—
I hesitate.

I answer.

"Sweetness."

"You're sure?
Sure it's not
the safety?"

"I'm sure.
Make me
a little
something
sweet.

But...
Something
little."

"Something little.
Something sweet."

Practiced hands go to work.
Kind eyes never stray
to the bottles.
She moves faster
than my eyes can follow.

Stoli. Other things.
Something red.
Into a shaker,
into a glass,
a stemmed glass,
a little one,
little more
than a mouthful,
little more
than a shot.

A little something.
Something dark,
something red,
something sweet.

What's in a Shirley Temple, anyway?
Cherry? Cherry, or something like it.

I sip it,
sweet and slow.

Something like cherries...
but not so much like them.

Dark,
red,
sweet.

Such a little something,
it's maybe four sips,
maybe six.

Who's counting, anyway?

Each a sip a moment,
each moment a month.
It's gone so soon.

"Good?" she asks.

"Perfect."

"What would you like now?"

What can I have now?
What can't I have now?

But I tell her,
"I can't stay.
I didn't expect...
my mother.
Expects me.
I told her,
I won't..."

"Be long?"

"Be long,"
I say.

Belong.

"We'll see," she says.
"I'll see you."

"Maybe you will."

"I will.
You'll be back."

"Maybe."

Maybe I will.

Maybe.

I will.
I know, I will
Come.
Again.

[ESC]

A woman walked into a bar.

She said, "Ouch!"

Wincing at the decor, the atmosphere, the cloying song on low-fidelity speakers about the conditional love for something called piña coladas, Grey resisted the urge to suspend the action and start fixing things. Or just removing them. This whole thing was Lisa's deal, and she recognized that Lisa had taken a step outside her own comfort zone even by suggesting it. If Lisa could try out immersion for her, she could suck it up and at least wait before she tried editing things.

Lisa was easy to find. She was at the bar at the other end of the room, wearing a red dress off her shoulders. It somehow managed to be out of place in a place that could not possibly admit to a dress code. She held a little red clutch purse. A drink stood on the bar next to her, something sickly green and oddly colloidal in a stemmed glass with sloped sides.

"Grey!" she called as Grey made her way over. "I guess, you, uh, you found the place, huh?"

"Yeah, uh... parking was a bitch, though?" Grey said, a little uncertainly. "You know, I'm sorry, I'm trying to be in character but I'm not sure what my character is. I'm not sure what kind of person comes to a place like this, or why."

"Just be yourself," Lisa said.

"Okay, but I'm not sure why *I* would come here, either," Grey said.

"You said you'd try the program with me."

"And I was excited that you wanted me to, but there are better programs. I mean, everything here is so fake," Grey said, looking at an oar on the wall that had clearly never been used and a sign that proclaimed it to be five o'clock somewhere. "Why design a virtual wall to look like it's painted to look like we're looking at the ocean when we could just be looking out at the ocean? We could be literally on the ocean. Literally. Or under it. In it. And what does it matter, what time it is somewhere else?"

"Please, give it a chance," Lisa said. "This is the latest in algorithmic dating."

"Wait, I thought you said dating other people isn't going to solve us," Grey said.

"Not dating other people."

"...so we're dating algorithms?" Grey said, looking around the bar at the men in loud shirts and cargo shorts, polo shirts and khakis, the women in everything up to and including very little. "They're certainly very... weathered-looking."

"We're letting the algorithm determine our date," Lisa said. "It read every bit of data in our public profiles and all the private profiles it can read — it has more licenses than we do, that's a big part of the cost — and it selected the perfect date for us."

"We paid money for this shit? Lisa, you know I make this kind of thing for a living. For fun. I could have made a better restaurant in about five minutes flat. More realistic. Or more fantastic. We could have dinner on the moon. We could get drunk in a tavern in a city of adventure. We could be anywhere in the world, *any* world, doing anything we want. So what are we doing here? Honestly. What are we doing?"

"I paid money — *my* money — for this program," Lisa said. "And I think it's worth a shot, okay? The testimonials are a little vague, but look, I read all the reviews I could find. They were very mixed..."

"Way to sell me on it, honey."

"Please don't interrupt. Not between bad and good," Lisa said. "Between great and meh. Nobody much really disliked it, but I noticed a difference between the people who said they loved it and the people who said it was just okay. The people who were raving, they said things like this app saved their marriage, it helped them rekindle their romance, it reminded them why they fell in love. The only people who said meh were..."

"Well?" Grey prompted after Lisa let the thought die, when she knew she wouldn't be interrupting. "What were they?"

"Happy," Lisa said. "They were happy, Grey. With their lives. With their relationship. With each other. Thought it was fun, nice, a good lark, interesting concept, a neat novelty, but didn't see the point of it."

"Well, I guess our relationship is great, because I don't see the point of it, either," Grey said. "Look, I know... I know we've got stuff to work on, but 'it saved our marriage' is just something people say. I bet you can find as many 'it saved our marriage!' reviews for sleep-in ear buds, mimetic mattresses, and waveform-inducing pillows. Or kitchen gadgets. Sexy underwear. Vibrators. You know, when you said you wanted an immersive VR date, I definitely had something else in mind."

"It wasn't just the reviews, Grey. I checked the public profiles, the ones that were verified, and they were from people on the verge of splitting up! Or already separated. I mean, some of them were in even worse shape than we are."

"Oh, wow," Grey said. "Thanks, Lisa. Thank you for that. That doesn't sting at all."

"Look, you don't want to talk about what's wrong," Lisa said. "But despite that, I don't think you're ready to give up on us."

"You make it sound like we're a sinking ship. We're not, are we? We're just going through a rough patch."

"I would argue, but then we'd be talking about it, and you'd shut down," Lisa said. "But look, we don't have to do that. That's the beauty of this! We can just follow the algorithm and see where it takes us."

"You think a date in a crappy, badly-rendered, turn-of-the-century bar is going to save our relationship?"

"It's already got you to admit we need saving!" Lisa said. "Anyway, it's not rendered poorly. This whole program is top-of-the-line. This is the highest level of fidelity possible."

"Then I say again: why does it all look so fake?"

"Because it is fake," Lisa said. "But it's a *real* fake. This is an exact replica of a real, authentic turn-of-the-century dining experience."

"There was a real place called 'Margaritaville'?"

"Loads of them, apparently," Lisa said. "A whole chain of them. Before people could download whole scenarios made to order, this is what they would do, you know, if they couldn't afford to travel. They'd go someplace that would bring the experience to them."

"So your magic marriage-saving algorithm thinks we need to learn what it was like to not be able to afford to go to the beach, back when you had to go to the beach to experience going to the beach?"

"I don't know what it wants," Lisa said. "Look, we can make whatever changes we want, we can even override the whole scenario, but I've read the reviews. I trust it. I want to see where it goes." She pushed the thick-stemmed cocktail glass with her greenish concoction in it down the bar towards Grey. "Here, try my margarita."

"It's a drink?" Grey took a sip. It was sweet and citrusy, with a real bite underneath. "Why do they salt the rim?"

"I don't know, but I find it adds something," Lisa said. "But yeah, it's a drink. So are piña coladas. Sorry that the song seems to be stuck on repeat."

"Is it? I thought it was just very repetitive."

"It is," Lisa said. "This particular restaurant chain was affiliated with a musician named Jimmy Buffett, but I guess they couldn't license his actual songs. From what I've gathered, this song's close enough to his oeuvre that it's thought to sort of sum it up, even though it's not his. So I think the atmospheric subroutine keeps pulling for the next song to play and all the more obvious choices get denied and it just goes down the list each time until it reaches something it can play."

"Which is... this," Grey said. Lisa nodded. Grey frowned. "You're trusting the fate of our relationship to a program that can't figure out how to not play the same song ten times in a row."

"It's got to be a low-percentage scenario," Lisa said. "It just happened that our ideal date is in a place with musical parameters it can't quite fulfill. If we were different people and had a different scenario, it wouldn't be doing this."

"So why don't we just do a different scenario?"

"Because it chose this for us. In spite of a technical quirk, it brought us here. I have to believe that means something. If we sit here long enough, sheer odds will eventually put another licensed song higher on the probability list than it. Eventually."

"And oh, what a treat that will be," Grey said. "Look, if this program knows everything about us, it would know that I hate this and it would know I would rather do anything else than sit here and listen to this song again. So how do you know that letting me change the program isn't what the algorithm wants?"

"I think there's got to be more to it than that," Lisa said. "Otherwise it would have just dumped us into a lobby or something. There must be something about this place that speaks to you."

"Yeah, it says 'get out'. Go to a real beach. Listen, even the song has better ideas. Make love at midnight? Dunes? Doesn't that sound better than this?"

"But the algorithm put us here. I think if we stay here, it might, I don't know, lead us to have some kind of breakthrough. Or something."

"And it did," Grey said. "You're always after me to tell you what I want and I always say I don't know, leave me alone. Well, now I know. This fake-ass crap on the walls and this insipid song have made me realize how much I want sex on the beach."

"Okay, we'll keep that in mind," Lisa said. "So how about we sit, we have dinner here, then we wander outside... maybe we'll find out the algorithm put us by a beach. Would that be enough to restore your trust in it? If it led you to realize that desire and then fulfilled it?"

"Why do we have to have dinner first?"

"Because we're talking! We're connecting," Lisa said. "We're arguing, but we're not... it's not a fight. Not like we used to have. It's a conversation. Look, at least have a drink with me."

"I don't want a drink."

"Then why did you order this?" the bartender said. He was holding a tall glass, slightly concave towards the middle, full of a peachish-orangish-reddish liquid.

"What is that?" Grey asked.

"Sex on the Beach," he said.

"[Escape]," Grey vocalized. The bartender froze. At the same moment, the fans overhead had stopped spinning, the crowd at the tables had stopped chattering, the repetitively light and breezy song had stopped playing in the background. The only things in the environment still moving and making noise were Lisa and herself, the players, the only things about the scenario that were really real. Knowledge of the program's command structure was now overlaid onto Grey's brain, like muscles she'd just grown but knew instinctively how to use. There were a lot of intricacies, but she didn't need to work in fine detail. "[Edit Environment: Remove NPCs: All]."

"What are you doing?" Lisa said. "This is what the algorithm wanted."

"And you're right, it got us talking," Grey said. "But now we've got people butting in, and that's no good. I don't want to drink some sticky sweet novelty drink and eat a virtual dinner that is an exact neurological recreation of something heated from a bag a hundred years ago. I'll stay and we can keep talking, but I'm not interested in any of this retro-chintz. Not when I know we could be experiencing the real thing."

"Fine, you want real?" Lisa said. "I'll just [Open: Related...] ...okay, here's a *real* restaurant in Old Key West, Florida."

The environment futzed out around them and then back into view, altered in ways both subtle and profound. They were now at a bar so weather-worn it might have been carved from driftwood, in an open-air eatery with a real blue sky overhead instead of a painted ceiling.

"Better?" Lisa asked.

"Better," Grey said.

"You know, I think that's the first time you've ever wanted something more real instead of less," Lisa said. "Maybe we're on the right track. Should we bring the crowd back?"

"I guess," Grey said. "Just turn interaction off. No, minimal. I don't want to have to spawn our own food and drinks."

"Okay," Lisa said. "Escape. Hmm. I think since you suspended the program, you've got to be the one who unpauses."

"[Escape]."

The scene chattered back to life. A hostess spotted them.

"Two?" she said. They nodded, and she led them to a table in the corner without another word.

"Look, you can actually see water from here," Grey said. "Actual water. I still want to do that sex on the beach thing later."

"Aren't you cocky?" Lisa said. "At least buy me dinner first."

Grey laughed. Lisa smiled.

"Look at us," Lisa said. "Joking around, flirting. It's like we're actually on a date again."

"Don't get all meta on me," Grey said. "You'll break the immersiveness. I really like this place."

"Yeah. Even the pigeons are pretty, somehow."

Grey turned to where Lisa was looking and saw a magnificent rooster strutting up the sidewalk.

"Talk about cocky," Grey said. "That's like an ornamental rooster."

Was there such a thing as an ornamental chicken? Had there been? Old Key West was wild, apparently.

"No, not that," Lisa said. "Look."

She pointed to where a trio of the most well-fed and fearless pigeons Grey had ever seen foraging for fallen food along the railing of the patio. They were close enough to see that they had jeweled iridescent highlights in their feathers. They apparently had no fear of people, though they did fall back a bit as the cockerel approached.

"Oh, yeah," Grey said. "Neat!"

"I'm surprised you're not freaking out," Lisa said. "You normally can't stand birds that close to where you're eating."

"Well, I mean, that's the power of the fantasy," Grey said. "We're looking at something real but I know it's all a generated experience. They can't really peck or scratch me. There's no consequences, if something gets contaminated or there's a disease."

"Now who's being meta?" Lisa said, and Grey stuck out her tongue. "But I guess now you maybe get the appeal of places like Margaritaville."

"I guess," Grey said. "I still like this place more. You know what I like best about it?"

"The playlist?" Lisa guessed.

"The playlist," Grey said. "I guess this is supposed to be beachy music. And you know, it does all sound a bit like that damned piña colada song. Certainly a lot of people singing about alcohol."

"It's not really about piña coladas, if you listen to it. It's more like a love song. The piña colada thing, the making love in the rain..."

"That's not even how it goes," Grey said, and she kind of hated herself for knowing that.

"It all kind of runs together and washes over you, though, doesn't it?" Lisa said. "I had to hear it about ten times before I even realized there's a story and it's not just about stuff this guy likes. But he's putting that stuff in his dating profile, you see, and then someone matches with him. It's about finding love."

"I guess it's deeper than I thought," Grey said. "And more modern, if they had public profiles."

"Oh, no, they're doing the whole thing on paper somehow? I don't know, I didn't follow all of that part. I wasn't actually trying to put it together, it just worms its way inside you, somehow."

"Doesn't it, though?" Grey said. "It's infectious. The one kind of infection you can get from immersion."

"The twentieth-century earworm," Lisa said. "I swear, I can hear it right now."

"Fuck! You can, it's just started playing again," Grey said. "[Escape]! [Escape]!"

"You just paused and unpaused it," Lisa said, laughing. "[Escape]."

"Sorry, I was desperate. I don't want to make a whole bunch of changes or anything, but I just really want to get the song out of the rotation. We'd only just... escaped... it."

"Hang on, this isn't like before. This is an organic part of the experience. Like, it's just as much an authentic part of the culture we're in as the songs before it, and it's not going to go on repeat. Why don't we just let it ride? You didn't remove the pigeons. Maybe you can appreciate it as part of the scenario."

"Fine, I guess it's already in my head. Maybe it'll be less annoying when I know the whole thing so it's not just the same lines repeating. What's this dude got against disco, anyway? It outlived his meager stylings, whatever you want to call them."

"It was probably on the way out when he wrote that," Lisa said. "Disco's always been kind of cyclical like that. Anyway, we can just sit and listen for a bit, and then resume our date. [Escape]."

Grey sat. She listened. She came to realize...

"SON OF A BITCH!" Grey shouted. Nobody around them reacted in the slightest. "It's not about new love! He's got someone! He's cheating, the dirty fucker. [Escape]! [Escape]! [Escape]! We're doing the beach thing, now."

"You can just hit it once," Lisa said. "It's very disorienting when you... whoa."

The setting changed around them, and Lisa was suddenly in a chair made of woven fabric stretched over a metal frame. It was almost pitch dark. Grey resumed the scene, but even then the sound and the scent on the breeze were the only things that told them they were by the ocean. The uneven ground under Grey's feet *felt like* sand, anyway.

"Okay, well, I think we can agree that the dunes at midnight is *clearly* some more of that cheating bastard's bullshit," Grey said.

"Maybe if we had less cloud cover and changed the moon phase," Lisa said. "Or added a bonfire or some fairy lights."

"No! No, I don't want to start fiddling around, or I might never stop," Grey said. "You know, once you start making little changes, who knows where it will lead? We can just change the time of day and leave everything else the same. Let's try mid-afternoon. No, sunset. Sunrise? I don't know what direction... hang on. [Escape]."

But the whole panoply of sex on the beach turned out to be some more of that same dude's bullshit. No matter what position they tried, how they arranged themselves or the topography or time of day, it was uncomfortable, frustrating, and unsatisfying. The sand got *everywhere*, and the whole thing was either wet and cold, or dry but cold enough that it somehow managed to feel wet, or burning hot. After half an hour of Grey trying to fine tune the sand's viscosity, coarseness, and temperature as preset variables independent of the rest of the scenario, she finally gave up.

"It's such a hot fantasy but the reality just doesn't work the way it does in my head," Grey said. "But you know, one advantage of living in the future is I'll bet this is a solved problem. We can probably go online and find where someone designed the perfect sex on the beach scenario, with the sand being sufficiently sand-like for most purposes so it feels real, but yielding and pliant or firm as needed for the good fucking."

"Is the two of us having sex on a pile of sand actually something that matters that much to you?" Lisa asked.

"Not really, no, it's not something I ever thought about in particular before the disco-hating douche put the idea in my head," Grey said. "But, I mean, isn't this kind of emblematic of, I don't know, everything? Like when we tried to have that picnic, and you cried because it wasn't exactly the way you pictured it in your head."

"I cried because you *yelled* and kicked the basket over," Lisa said.

"I *nudged* the basket with my foot because a moving wall of ants was about to envelop it and I raised my voice because I was alarmed by the ants," Grey said. "And even before that it wasn't exactly a picnic. The day looked nice but it was hot as a blast furnace. There were all those little biting flies. When the wind shifted, we suddenly realized the nice picturesque pond smelled like algae and rotting fish."

"And after that, you went into your room and didn't talk to me for three days," Lisa said. "Retreated into immersion. When you finally had to come out, it didn't get any better. You were so tense. If I tried to talk to you, you snapped. You were so annoyed with me, I wondered... I wondered why you didn't leave. And the longer it went on, the more I wondered why I didn't."

"I was frustrated!" Grey said. "I wasn't annoyed with you, I was just... annoyed, and then I was still annoyed when you talked to me. If anything, I was less annoyed when I talked to you, because I was talking to you. When I had to come out for meals, I was actually glad for the distraction. But I guess you couldn't see the baseline level for comparison."

"What were you so annoyed about? The ants?"

"It wasn't annoyance as much as frustration," Grey said. "I was actually... I was working on something. I was trying to fix the picnic. The same way I did with the sand, just now. But it wasn't *just* the sand, or the ants, it was everything. You know, you can design an experience from the ground up but then it's always going to be a bit abstract or surreal, even if you're using procedural generation. Or you can start with a realistic environment and try to edit its parameters. It's really hard to take a real scene and make it perfect. Feel the warmth of the sun without the heat of the air. The breeze carrying the smell of the wildflowers but not the rot. You can start with easy obvious things like birds that sing but don't poop and bees that buzz but don't sting or land on your drink, but when you start editing the environment, every little thing you change reveals or causes other little things you'll need to change, and if you change too much the whole thing feels fake and you have to start undoing. I wanted it to be real, but perfect. I never found the right balance."

"You never told me," Lisa said.

"Yeah, well, at first it was going to be a surprise," Grey said. "Because I thought it would be so easy. I went in there with a list of things that needed fixing and I fixed them. But when that didn't work, I tried to fix the fixes, and then I had to fix it some more, and the whole thing just became a mess, and then you started getting upset. I was probably too invested in what I was doing, but at first I thought if I could just get it right and show you, surprise you, then you'd be happy again and it would all be worth it. Then I guess I lost sight of why I was doing it a little, I started... I started to sort of hate you. I don't like saying that. I didn't hate you. But going outside and talking to you stopped feeling like a break and started feeling more like an ordeal. There was the real you, who hovered and needled and was never happy with me, and there was the you I was doing it for, the one in my head, the one who would understand and be so pleased with me when I finished."

"I wasn't unhappy with you," Lisa said. "I was unhappy *without* you. I was desperate for you, Grey. You were so closed off. Even before the picnic, you'd do that thing. Retreat. Wall yourself off. Hide in your room and dive into your latest obsession, barely look at me, barely speak to me. It just got worse, after the picnic."

"Eventually I realized I couldn't finish it, couldn't get it right and I was so afraid... I was afraid you were going to leave me, and I didn't have any way to stop you," Grey said. "The one thing I put my faith in, the thing I thought would fix everything, it was a bust. All that time, all those days, weeks..."

"Months," Lisa said.

"If you say so. All those months wasted. I was sure I was going to lose you."

"I thought I already had lost you," Lisa said. "I don't need things to be perfect, okay?"

"You always freak out when something doesn't go the way you planned it, the way you expected it to."

"I... have to take some time to adjust," Lisa said. "From my point of view, you freak out a little when I try to take a breath to process a change. If you think it's something you can fix, you spring into action and then you're focused on solving the problem instead of whatever we're meant to be doing, and if you're afraid you can't, you... get mad."

"It's more frustration than anger."

"I think it's more fear," Lisa said. "You're afraid that if you can't solve whatever's wrong then I'll be unhappy."

"Is there something wrong with wanting my partner to be happy?"

"I can't be happy all the time," Lisa said. "And I don't have to be unhappy for long. Things aren't always going to go my way. I can deal with that. And when I can't... well, I can deal with the fact that I can't. *We* can deal with it. We're a couple. It's not your job to make me happy, or mine to make you. It's our job to make our life together."

"Make it what?"

"Just... make it," she said. "You know? Share the good times, have someone with us in the bad. Look back and laugh at all the things that went wrong. You know, before you got upset, what I thought about the picnic... what I told myself to calm myself down... was that at least it would be a funny story. I thought we'd be talking about it for years. Instead, we never talked about it, and as the years went on, we hardly talked about anything else. You never even told me you were trying to fix it."

"Well, at first it was a surprise, and then I guess it was a shame," Grey said. "I haven't thought about it in more than a year, probably, and before that I hardly ever did. Though, every time I did..."

"You got a flash of resentment?" Lisa said. "It kind of showed. You'd just twinge and get this look on your face, like a dark cloud out of nowhere."

"Yeah, I guess I did," Grey said. "I thought you weren't happy with the real thing and you'd never be happy with the recreation..."

"*You* weren't happy with it," Lisa said. "I didn't know about it.

"It's possible I was projecting a bit," Grey said.

"That's what happens if you don't talk about things," Lisa said. "They just build up inside you. They fester. They bubble up at the worst possible times, and poison everything."

"I just always felt like if I started talking about it, I'd think about how frustrating it was and I'd feel it all over again and then I'd just... start screaming, and never stop," Grey said. "You've got such a low tolerance for anything that looks like anger, even when it's not about you."

"It's better if you talk about it, so I know it's not about me," Lisa said.

"Well, we're talking now," Grey said. "And... okay, I'd be lying if I said I'm not feeling a little sore right now. You know? I understand I've been a bitch sometimes but I think you're downplaying your, uh... I'm going to say coping problems. If I got a little too pro-active with trying to handle things as they come up, it's because I've seen you fall to pieces when I don't."

"Fair," Lisa said. "But, that's not every time. And if you've seen me fall to pieces, you know I can eventually pull myself back together."

"Maybe... maybe I'm afraid of what would happen if you can't," Grey said. "It might be a low percentage scenario, but the cost would be way too high."

"You're not going to lose me from a bad date," Lisa said. "Not if you don't want to. Not if you don't push me away."

35

"I'm really glad to hear you say that," Grey said. "Because I think we can agree this one's been a disaster."

"...yeah," Lisa said. "I mean, we're finally talking but the program hasn't even been running for the past ten minutes."

"What do you say we blow this popsicle stand and I can show you some of my own work?" Grey said. "I was serious about the moon restaurant thing. We can do that."

"Are you pushing that one in particular just so you can make a joke about how the food is good but there's no atmosphere?"

"...not *just* for that reason, no."

"Because, actually, if you still have it, I'd like to see the picnic program," Lisa said.

"Are you sure? Because it's a disaster," Grey said. "Like having an afternoon stroll through the uncanny valley. I was in the middle of ripping it apart and putting it back together when I stopped working on it. Like, parts of it are a horror show."

"I'd still be happy to see your work," Lisa said. "I mean, I think I'd appreciate the amount of effort you put into it."

"Okay, so we'll log off and I'll go put my scenario in our house cloud," Grey said. "While I'm doing that, you can leave this nightmare of a program its first one-star review."

"I don't know if I would do that?" Lisa said. "I don't think it's that bad. I think maybe we're just not the target audience. I mean, all those people who said it fixed their relationship... we fixed our own. Which I think means that even though we hit a bad patch and sort of drifted out of sync, underneath it all, the fundamentals of it were still really strong."

"That's actually a really reassuring thing to realize," Grey said. "Even if it's basically what I said at the beginning."

"So I think maybe I'll leave it a three-star review, like all those people who didn't really see the point of it," Lisa said. "I'm sure it's not a bad program, it just didn't know what to do with a pair like us. But even still, it shook us out of our routine, didn't it?"

"I think you did that," Grey said. "That was you. And I'm so glad you did. Okay. Going to log off now. Do you want me to wait for you, or...?"

"Go ahead and get things started," Lisa said. "Then afterwards, maybe you could revert it to the original and we could try our date again."

"Really?"

"Really. After everything we've been through, I think I deserve a taste of champagne."

"So you want the whole thing, ants and all?"

"Maybe just leave out the ants."

Walk Briskly

The funeral home is very old, old enough that it still has an old-style chapel. That's where we're holding what is still called the viewing.

The podium on which sits the now-traditional portfolio album is situated in the middle of a recessed nook that was obviously designed to hold something a bit larger than a person in repose, and which now holds something a bit smaller than the average end table.

I'm being a bit clinical about it all partly because I wish to remain detached from the scene, and partly because I am detached, whether I want to be or not.

The jungle of flowers flanking the photo display does nothing to disguise how small it is. It swallows it up.

From a certain angle, it looks like my mother's unnaturally youthful face is peering at me from out of a monstrous hybrid rose bush.

It is not a pleasant or comfortable idea, all things considered.

I turn away. It's not easy to detach myself from that image.

My grandmother isn't any happier with the state of things. She handled the arrangements. She picked the funeral home. It apparently has some history that I don't remember with her side of our family.

I wonder how many times has she been here, before?

How many times, after?

How long would it take a person to get used to a change of that magnitude?

I don't know.

The world I live in is the only one I've ever known.

My uncles have been trying to keep my grandmother calm for a good twenty minutes. Their results have varied.

"But I just wish I had another chance to see her," she is saying when I tune back in. "Would that really be so much?"

"Ma, the law's the law," my Uncle Mike says.

"It wouldn't be her anyway," Uncle Jeff says. "You know a body's just a body. Anyway, is that how you want to remember her? The pictures are better."

"The pictures are pictures!" Grandmother yells. "She's my only daughter!"

"Geez, quiet down, Ma," Mike says. "People are gonna..."

"People know she's grieving," Jeff says. "That's what this is. Grief. It's okay. Ma, you know it would break her heart if she knew you took that kind of risk. You know how careful she was all the time."

"You mean she was afraid all the time," Mike says. "And she wasn't happy if everyone else wasn't."

That's when I turn away.

* * * * * * * * * *

"Walk!"

This is what she'd yell whenever I headed out the door. It didn't matter where in the house she was, or whether I'd told her I was going out. She'd sense the front door opening, zip to the doorway nearest to the front hall, and yell out the reminder.

"I know," I'd call back over my shoulder.

"Don't run!"

"I KNOW!"

I did know. Everybody knew. Just like, sometimes, everybody ran, because no matter how brave we all acted around the schoolyard, we still got scared a bit at a rustling in the ditches or when we saw something staring eyelessly out of a hedge.

There was no need to run. None of them could. Most of them could barely walk. But at the same time, there was no real reason not to run. The point was to get away, right? Running was safer than walking. As for the risks...

"That's how you trip," my mother would say.

"But I'm still faster even if I trip," I said back to her, once. "If they're not close enough to grab me when I start running, they're not going to be any closer when I fall!"

"The one you know about won't be," she said. "They hunt in packs, remember?"

"Mother!" I said. "There haven't been packs for years!"

"There are occasional packs still," she said. "It doesn't even have to be a pack. It could just be two of them, the one you see and the one you don't. Anyway, it really only takes one. What if you trip and twist your ankle? What if you break your leg?"

"I'll still drag myself faster than it can," I said.

"Oh? Have you ever had a broken leg? Remember when you broke your finger? You almost blacked out."

"I could still trip if I'm walking."

"But it's all about odds," she said. "It's all about risk. When you're running, you can't keep your eyes on the ground. You don't have as much time to react when something comes up. You can't stop yourself if your foot snags on something. And what happens if you wind up running right into a dead end?"

"We don't live in a *labyrinth*," I said. It was a new word to me at that point, and I was very proud of it. Probably a bit too proud, or else I wouldn't have dared to say that, as sure of myself as I was.

I don't remember exactly what my mother said in response to that. I do remember I was less proud of my vocabulary afterwards.

I never argued with her about that again. I still didn't think she was right about running. If it was about odds, then who was to say that it wasn't riskier to spend more time in the area? If there might be more than one, then wouldn't it be better to get out of there before they could surround me?

But even if I didn't think running was as dangerous as she made it out to be, I recognized that there was a different kind of danger in pushing her too far.

In all honesty, the danger posed by the amblers was distant and abstract compared to the danger posed by pressing my mother's buttons. I had no experience with being dragged down by an ambulatory corpse, but I had been grounded.

Anyway, the debate about running had only been a side point in an older, longer-running argument about the way to deal with things like amblers in the first place.

* * * * * * * * * *

"Hey there, Safety Tip," my cousin Brian says.

"I've asked you not to call me that," I say.

"Ah, hell," he says. "I've been calling you that for years. Everybody in school did! What else am I supposed to call you?"

"My name. Anything else. Just don't call me *that* today."

"What's so special about today?"

I stare at him. I know he's making fun of me, but I can't tell if this is part of the tease or not. I don't know which would be crueler.

"My mother is dead," I say. It's all I can do to get the words out. I expect them to come tumbling from my mouth in a rising roar, but when I hear my voice, it is tiny, thin, and piercing. I want my words to push him away, but I can see on his face he doesn't even feel it.

I turn and walk briskly away.

* * * * * * * * * *

My mother always did love her safety tips.

Look both ways before crossing the street. Don't go in the water for a half hour after eating. Stop, drop, and roll if you catch on fire. Stop, look, and listen when you get to the train tracks.

Her favorite, of course, was the famous WALK.

Every time she shouted "walk" to me as I was heading out the door, I knew she didn't just mean "walk" but "W.A.L.K."

I knew this because for the longest time, she would give me the whole spiel before letting me go out alone:

"W: WALK briskly. A: Stay ALERT. L: Keep your eyes LOW. K: KNOW the area."

That's what you did if you encountered an ambler. That's what you were supposed to do, anyway.

Don't approach.

Don't engage.

Don't stop and watch it stumble around towards you.

Don't laugh at it, no matter how helpless and harmless it looks.

Don't stop and take a picture of it.

Definitely don't try to get a picture with it.

Almost everyone else in my class had a picture of themselves with an ambler in the background. Polaroids, mostly, because those didn't have to be developed. The kids who had actual film photographs were the coolest kids with the coolest parents, the ones who would let them have everything and let them do anything.

Justin Peterson was one of those kids.

He had a picture with his arm around one, though it was dead. I mean, it had been rendered inert again. He'd shot it between the eyes and then propped it up for a picture, which his dad took.

He'd been a hero to the whole school, once.

For a while, everyone had wanted to be him.

* * * * * * * * * *

"I'm told your mother died peacefully," a blonde woman wearing a red pillbox hat with a veil of netting on it tells me. "And that she passed without incident."

"Yeah," I say.

I've been told that, too.

Everybody keeps telling me that. They clasp my hand in theirs, give me firm, unblinking eye contact, and tell me the news that I had been given long before them: my mother's body went into the crematorium peacefully and still.

Why do they tell you this? Why do they think you need to know? Dead is dead, even now, or at least gone is gone. My mother is every bit as gone as if something *had* tried to beat and claw its way out of the box.

Anyway, what do they tell the people whose loved ones did turn unexpectedly? If it's supposed to bring peace to know that it didn't happen, what do they tell the family when it does happen? Nothing?

Then I know, with a certainty: they passed without incident. Like an angel. Like a sleeping angel.

Of course they do.

"What a blessing!" the pillbox lady says.

"Yeah," I agree.

"I had nightmares about my Albert, before he went into the fire," she continues. My eyes dart around the room looking for an escape, but I know I'll find none. I came to this corner to escape. It seemed like the last safe place for me to stand. "They tell me that they can't feel anything, that it's not really them anymore, but what if they're wrong? What if they're wrong? They still don't know why it happens, and I mean, people used to think cows don't feel anything. We don't really know anything, do we?"

"No, we don't."

* * * * * * * * * *

The first thing I asked for when my mother said I was old enough to go out by myself was a sword. Sherry Morgan had one that she said was Japanese. Her grandfather had brought it back from the war, she said, and now it was hers. Everybody thought it was the coolest.

I liked it because I thought its curved, single-edged blade would impress my mother. What could be safer than that?

"Don't be silly," she said. "What good is a sword for?"

"Sherry says it can cut right through bone and everything," I said.

"What sounds safe about that?" she said.

"Mom, it's not even sharp like a razor," I said. "You have to, you know, swing it. Hard."

"Then it's not going to do you much good at your age, is it?" she said. "Anyway, you don't have any reason to cut one up. All that's good for is getting seven kinds of yuck on you, and it doesn't even stop them."

"I could cut off its arms and legs and then go for the head," I said. "Sherry Morgan says she's killed lots of them."

"You don't kill an ambler, sweetie," my mother said. "They aren't alive."

46

"They're kind of alive?" I said. "Mr. Grossman says they're undead."

"That is superstition," she said. "They're just... a thing that happens. Like a storm, or an avalanche, or a sickness. And speaking of sickness, the last thing you want to do is smack into them with a sword. Who knows what germs you'll splatter yourself with?"

"Mom, you can't *catch it*," I said.

"That's what they say, but no one knows what causes it," she said. "And even if you can't, you can catch other things. A rotting body is a perfect incubator for disease."

"I'd be careful!" I said.

"Showing off with a sword is the opposite of careful," she said. "I'll get you something you can use to keep them off of you and get away. That's the goal. Just get away."

When she told me she'd get me a pike instead, I hadn't known what she meant. Looking it up in the school library, I'd found pictures of wicked looking medieval weapons that looked like a spear had a baby with an axe. It wasn't a shotgun. It wasn't a handgun. It wasn't a chainsaw. It wasn't a sword. It wasn't any of the things that I'd ever wished for, but I didn't care. That just meant no one I knew had anything like it.

It meant that for once, I was going to be the cool kid.

When she actually brought it home, I was horrified. It was nothing like the pictures from the book. It reminded me of a whaler's harpoon, or at least what I imagined one would look like, only the end of it wasn't pointed or hooked at all. It was just a broad, flat metal thing, kind of like a boat oar. The patented safety tip, the package had called it.

My mother had loved her safety tips.

"If the goal's to get away, why not just get me a sword?" I said. "At least then I could run away!"

I knew the words were a mistake as soon as I'd said them, but it was too late to take them back and I didn't have the speed or eloquence needed to explain that I'd meant it in the sense of retreating, sensibly, at a safe speed.

"Don't. You. Dare."

I think I knew then and there that my fate was sealed, that I'd be stuck with the pike forever.

"I didn't mean it like that," I said.

"You don't run from them. If you see them, you walk away from them. Walk briskly. The pike is only for when one gets in your way, when one lurches around a corner or sneaks up on you."

"How are they going to sneak up on me? Everyone says they barely know we're here anymore! You practically have to step on one to get bitten."

"Those are the old ones," she said. "New ones pop up all the time, and they're still a bit quicker, and they have better senses."

"They still can't exactly sneak," I protested. "They're not smart like that."

"No, but they're very quiet and they're very patient," she said. "Anyway, if you're so sure they can't get close, then why do you care if you have a sword or a pike? You shouldn't need to use it very often."

"Then can I just leave it at home?"

"You were the one who wanted a way to defend yourself."

"I wanted a weapon!" I said. "I want to fight them!"

"There's nothing to fight! They aren't exciting! They aren't enemies to defeat! They're just something to avoid when we can, and deal with when we can't! That's what you have to do."

* * * * * * * * * *

They call what happens next the remembrance, though I know I won't remember much of it.

While her brothers and co-workers get up and talk about the kind of person they think she was, I'm looking at my mother's face in the big round oval frame that dominates the display.

The pictures were chosen from all times of her life. The biggest one is the one that I guess people thought would best represent her.

It wouldn't have been my choice, and not just because I have a hard time remembering when she ever looked that young. Her cheeks are too rosy. Her lipstick waxy-thick. I know she looks happy, but only because I already know what she looked like when she was happy.

Her smile isn't right. It isn't real. She's smiling because that's what you do, when someone points a camera at you.

But she's happy underneath it.

I don't know what a corpse looked like, lying in a coffin with its face made up by a mortician and fixed into the best approximation of a relaxed expression that can be wrung from a corpse. I've read old books, though, where people talk about how such faces are unfamiliar, artificial.

I feel that way looking at the picture of my mother. I couldn't guess the context from which the portrait was cropped. The background is an almost white sky. She's smiling for the camera, with no idea that this forced, fixed expression is going to be her death mask.

* * * * * * * * *

"Take your pike if you're going out," my mother said when she saw I was heading for the door without it.

"They just did a sweep yesterday," I said.

"And they always miss one," she said. "Watch the news and you'll see. The day after a sweep is always when someone gets taken. Because it makes people careless, you see. Someone always dies after a sweep."

"They do a sweep every month," I said. "If someone died every time..."

"Oh, for heaven's sake, I don't mean just here. But somewhere. Anywhere. It could be here. Take your pike."

I sighed and lifted the long, unwieldy pole off its wall mounting.

"If you want to keep me safe from amblers, you should have got me a gun," I said. I thought my logic was foolproof. "It's got a lot longer reach than a big, heavy stick."

"Are you kidding?" she said. "A gun is way more dangerous than an ambler."

"Isn't that the point?" I said.

"Do you know how many people get shot every day by accident? Do you know how many people a day shoot themselves?"

Probably not even one, I thought. It couldn't happen that often or people wouldn't make guns. They wouldn't be allowed.

I didn't know the answer, though I did know that I was on a losing track.

"I don't even know how I'm supposed to kill an ambler with this thing," I said instead.

"You aren't supposed to kill them," she said. "First, they're already dead. Second, that's why we have patrols. You're supposed to get away from them. If one's in your way, you push it back or you knock it down. Sweep..."

"Sweep the knees!" I said. "I know!"

"You get it down, and then you..."

"Then I walk away. *Briskly.*"

* * * * * * * * * *

My name is called.

I remember having been told that I should probably say something, and I remember that I had said in response that I would like that.

I hadn't given it any more thought.

That's just what you do when your mother dies, right?

It's never happened to me before and it would never happen again, but even an hour ago I couldn't imagine that I wouldn't want to stand up in front of a room of mixed family and strangers, that I wouldn't have anything inside me to say to them.

* * * * * * * * * *

Justin Peterson got his throat torn out when I was fourteen. He'd been hunting in the woods, supposedly for deer but probably not really.

He turned.

There's no rule that says getting killed by one always turns you into one, if there are any rules at all. It seems to happen more often that way, though. Some people think there is just a correlation between dying violently and alone and turning, but other people say that's just anecdotal. They say it seems that way because people who died in accidents in the middle of nowhere never get cremated.

I don't know.

I do know that when the thing that had been his body stumbled onto the field during an outdoor day in gym class, I was the last one to know it had been him. I turned, and I walked briskly towards the school, taking the long way around the big sloping hill up to the parking lot, because I might slip. I heard my classmates' laughter turn to screams and resisted the urge both to look back and to run.

Most of them were okay, physically. They were screaming because they recognized who it had been. Some of the jocks tried to tackle it and bash its brains in. One of them got a bad bite on his arm. He needed stitches and antibiotics, but he lived. His reputation did a 180 overnight, though. No one ever quite believed that it wasn't infectious. He went from being one of the coolest kids in school to a total pariah.

It wasn't just that the other kids were afraid of him. He'd get knocked down in the hall, have things thrown at his head. People would shuffle past him, moaning in the way that amblers never moan but people always act like they do.

I didn't understand it. I still don't. Everyone acted like at any moment he might turn into a monster and kill us all, but they didn't act like he was a *threat*. They acted like he was weak. I asked my mother about it, not because she'd understand but because I didn't have anyone else to ask.

"Fear does that to people sometimes," she said. "It brings out the worst in people. That's part of why it's so important not to be afraid."

"But you don't act like that."

"Sweetheart, that's because I'm not afraid," she said. "And I don't want you to be afraid, either. I don't want you to think you have to be afraid."

"Then why do I have to carry a stupid pike around, if I'm not supposed to be afraid? Why do I have to know all the rules? And why are you always checking on me, always hassling me about them? Why all the stupid safety tips?"

"There are things we do when things are scary, so that we won't be afraid," she said. "It would be terrifying to go down the road at sixty miles an hour if there weren't seat belts and brakes and signal lights and, and... safety features. We have all those things, and we have rules of the road, and because we can count on them to keep us safe, we don't have to be afraid."

"But people still die in car accidents, don't they?"

"They do."

"And people still get killed by amblers."

"Yes," she said. "Yes, they do. I'm afraid they probably always will."

"You *are* afraid!" I said. I'm not sure if I felt triumphant or terrified at having caught her in this contradiction. "You said you're not!"

"I don't have to be," she said. "Love, things—people—aren't just one way or another. Sometimes I get scared when I'm driving, too! The important thing is that it doesn't become all that I am, that the things I feel don't overwhelm the things I know, like how to drive safely. The important thing is that you don't panic."

* * * * * * * * * *

"My mother," I say, "always kept me safe."

I know these words are inadequate. I know I should be explaining, elaborating... saying something about how she knew it was a scary world, and she didn't hide that from me, but she always made sure I had the tools to deal with it.

I should be saying that "safe" didn't mean I wouldn't die, though I didn't. It didn't mean she didn't worry every time I went out the door, but that she could let me go out the door.

None of these words will come, though. They won't form up into ranks inside my head and I can't make them march out of my mouth.

"She wasn't afraid," I say. "She taught me not to be afraid. I love her, and I miss her... and I'll always miss her... but I still know I don't have to be afraid."

People are looking at me like they're not sure if I'm finished. Have I said enough?

"That's all I have to say," I say. "There isn't anything else..."

There's some awkward, scattered clapping, which weirds me out because I didn't expect it. Were people clapping at the other speakers? I get out from behind the lectern and head down the aisle. I don't go back to my seat. I need air, but more than that, I need to be somewhere else, anywhere else, just as fast as I can safely get there.

I fumble out the claim ticket for the coat check and thrust it with shaking hands to the attendant, who peers at the scribbled scrawl underneath the description.

"It's the pike," I say. "Seven and a half feet long, with a safety tip."

"Right," he says. "I saw that in the corner. Hang on. You know, I didn't know anyone still carries these. Sure, you could brain a thing hard with it, but it's so awkward to swing. There's got to be easier ways to take out an ambler."

"I'm sure there are," I say. "But I don't have to take them out. I just have to get away."

"Well, an ambler alert just came through. They say the threat level for tonight is elevated, so if you're not looking to fight, you'd best be ready to run. Can I call you a cab?"

"No, thank you," I say, sniffling. "I'll walk. Briskly."

The Die Is Cast

I live in a place I cannot leave, and there is a point past which I cannot go.

...

That's not the truth, or not the whole truth. I live in a place I dare not leave, and there is a point past which I dare not go. That's more accurate. That's the truth.

It sounds so melodramatic when I say it, either way, but even more so when I say it the true way. I think I'd be embarrassed to say it, if there were only ever anyone around to hear me.

There's never anyone around to hear me.

I was in a writing group once, a sort of circle, and there was a guy who would jump on anyone who said "never".

"Never is never true," he'd say, or maybe it was "never makes itself true." His arguments didn't make sense to me, and maybe that's why I can never remember exactly what they were.

I tried looking up online to see if anyone else had the same rule, or a better way of explaining it. Not because I thought he was right, but because I wanted to know for myself exactly how he was wrong. The problem is that if you search for any combination of "never", "use" or "say", and "writing", you get literally every writing tip under the sun in the results.

Refining the search to try to make it explicit that it's about the word "never" brings up relationship advice (where "always" and "never" make for non-productive accusations) or cheery "never say never" aphorisms.

The working theory I've cobbled together over the years is that this guy went to couple's counseling or a relationship coach and got dinged for saying his partner never did this and never did that, and so he internalized the idea that never was just a bad word to use, period.

As explanations go... it makes sense, it's plausible, and it could be true. That should be enough, given that the actual answer isn't something I can know, and doesn't matter at all.

But the guy's bad advice got under my skin and rankled me. How stubborn and self-assured he was about it frustrated me. I haven't seen him for more than a decade, haven't seen anyone from the group for almost seven years, and yet I'll still randomly flash back to him when I say or think the word "never".

If I could get out of here, I think one of the things I'd do is hunt him down, if he's still around, and ask him where the hell he got this idea from.

It's not that nobody in the group ever challenged him. But since he acted like his ideas were self-evident and had no interest in changing his mind, everybody just sort of gave up. Let him be. Worked around him.

Listen to me ramble. None of this has anything to do with anything. It would be embarrassing, prattling on like this about ancient, petty slights, if anyone were around to hear me.

Nobody is ever around to hear me.

I live in a quiet house on a quiet street. It was always a quiet house. If anything, it seems louder now than it ever was, when there was a world outside to contrast it to.

It was not always a quiet street, or at least, not always so quiet, but now the street is silent. Deathly quiet. The house booms in comparison to the street.

I don't know when the world outside started to fall away. That's the plain truth. I don't. I was always good at tuning things out, ignoring intrusive sounds, working around inconveniences. I arranged my life so that I could stay buttoned up inside my quiet house for days at a time, if I needed to, and then I found reasons to need to, and cut out reasons to leave.

I'd always hated ringing phones. I had been one of the first to cut the cord when landlines went out of fashion, and my friends knew better than to call me out of the blue.

They'd text first, and often only text. They texted more often than I texted them, even more often than I texted them back.

Gradually, they'd texted less and less.

Were they my friends? They were friendly towards me. But they were never close, and I never completely convinced myself they did more than tolerate me.

Never, never.

I could never get away from that word.

Couldn't ever

I remember the day I woke up late and thought I must have woken up early, because there were no voices outside my window and no sounds of traffic. The sun was up and the sky was blue, but there was a pre-dawn hush to the world.

I wondered briefly if something had happened... no specific "something" in mind, it just seemed like the thing to wonder in that moment... and then a rusty pickup truck rolled slowly down the street and the spell was broken.

And the next day it was quiet again when I woke up, but I didn't make a big deal out of it, because I'd already done that once and felt foolish.

I remember weeks of feeling like I was ordering groceries less and less, and running out for them even less still. I remember times I surprised myself by finding the milk jug full or an entire carton of eggs when I was sure I'd almost used them up.

I remember the day I was sure that the trash collection had skipped me, because the truck didn't wake me up at three in the morning. But when I went outside, the cans were empty.

Unmoved, or else very neatly put back exactly where they had been left.

But empty.

That was the day that I looked at the calendar and realized I had not left my house in three weeks, and had not had a delivery or spoken to another human being in all that time.

I checked my phone and realized that my last text message was a good month and a half before.

I checked my kitchen and found that the cupboards and fridge were comfortably stocked.

I didn't know what to do with this information, with any of it.

So... I didn't.

Do.

Anything.

The street had been getting quiet. The world had been getting quieter. When I had gone outside to check the trashcans, something had been definitely wrong, something beyond the solitude and the silence.

Something that had made me feel uncomfortable, something that had driven me back inside.

I knew this, but I didn't want to know it, didn't want to think about it, and above all, didn't want to go back outside to try to figure out what it was.

So I sort of hunkered down inside my head for a couple of days, the way I so often had, and tried to forget about it.

It didn't work very well.

I never saw anyone from my windows, not even the upstairs triple bay windows that afforded such a clear view of the street. I never saw any signs of life, human or other animal. No sight or sound of traffic anywhere. The cars that were parked on our residential side street remained parked on our residential side street.

The lights in the other buildings that were left on stayed on. The ones that would have been turned on and off remained off.

I never saw anything *wrong* from my windows, just everything I would expect to see if I were somehow the only person around.

It was three days before I decided I needed to go and see what was happening outside my door. It would have been easy to talk myself out of it. I wasn't short on supplies. There was no physical discomfort or danger. I had everything I needed in my narrow little townhouse: food, water, meds. Everything.

The lights were on. The internet was working. I still had cell service.

This is the thing that makes me feel desperately foolish now. I still had cell service, at that point. I still had the internet. I could have called someone. I could have texted. I could have emailed any of my friends or just posted on their Facebook wall.

I could have asked someone to come visit me, swing by. Pick me up for a night on the town.

I feel like if I had done that then, I wouldn't be trapped now. I feel like the lines of communication I had left to me at that point were like a lifeline being spooled out from the world that was leaving me behind, and all I needed to do was grab hold of them and I would have been pulled along with the world, rescued before I had a chance to sink irretrievably below the surface of... whatever it was I was trapped in.

Maybe it wouldn't have worked. Maybe my connection to the world was one way. Maybe I could read Facebook posts and receive emails but not send anything.

I don't know. I don't know how that would have even worked. Every time you visit a webpage, you're sending information. The fact that I could browse the world wide web meant my computer was capable of sending a request to a DNS server. It could present credentials, stored login information. Information was going outward from me to the world.

So it seems like probably it should have worked, if I'd wanted to send someone an email. If I'd dared to.

But I can't fully convince myself that the logic under which these things normally operated was in operation for me, even back then.

Still. I wish I'd tried. If I'd tried, even if it had failed, I would know. I would know that it wasn't my fault, and I would have that much more information about the situation I'm in now.

At the time, I let myself be convinced that the internet meant that things were mostly okay, mostly normal. Just a little weird. Just a little uncanny. Just a little impossible.

That made me complacent, but it also, I think, gave me the courage to actually go outside and figure out what was so freaky, that I couldn't see from my windows but that I had felt from the sidewalk.

I got the weird, unsettling feeling as soon as I stepped outside. It was different than the anxiety of knowing... thinking... I was going to face something freaky. I'd felt that before I even opened the door.

I knew I was seeing something wrong as soon as I was clear of the frame. I didn't know what it was. I couldn't see what I was seeing.

I looked around, up the street and down it. My street was a through street, but a little side one, a shortcut cutting an angle between main drags not far from the downtown area of the small city where I lived.

The asphalt was cracked and riddled with potholes. The sidewalks were worse, but they were all pretty clean. The people had always taken care of what they could, even when the city wouldn't.

There were still no signs of life. No bugs. No birds. No moving vehicles. No dogs.

No people.

I didn't want to head too far from the comfort of my own front door to begin with, so I decided to head across the street and look in a few windows.

I was also half-convinced that as soon as I set foot in the street, a car would come zooming out of nowhere and almost run me over, just like in that movie with the meteor zombies.

Tempting fate, or calling its bluff, or something.

It didn't happen, though.

I crossed the street without incident, my feeling of dread intensifying as I took each step farther from my home and closer to the big plate glass picture window of the antique store that occupied the ground floor of the aging apartment building across the street.

It was dark inside, dark and wrong. I couldn't say how, but I didn't like what I was seeing. Didn't trust it. The sign in it was still flipped around to closed, as it had been ever since I'd started paying attention to it through my own windows.

I could see the rocking horse and the big wooden nutcracker on display, and the three big trophies in a row between them, just as I had seen them from my window.

I couldn't see anything beyond them.

I got up close, and the situation didn't change much. I couldn't see past them into the shop. It was dark, more than dark. I tried looking in at an angle, different angles, but couldn't see anything else. It was like the cold sunlight didn't penetrate more than a few inches through the glass, wouldn't slant in and light up anything around the window display.

I looked down, and saw that the shadows were so deep and complete they cut off the bases of the trophies, the soldier's feet, and the bottom of the rocking horse's runners. It was like they just stopped. Like they'd been cut off.

Light didn't work like that.

Darkness didn't work like that.

Nothing worked like that.

I backed away from that window, and looked in a few others of the businesses and residences on the ground floor across the street from me.

Everywhere I looked, it was all the same. I could see just inside the window, and no further. The farther I went in either direction, the worse it was. I didn't have to go too far up the street before I couldn't even see the inside parts of the window frames, before the glass itself became weirdly dark and indistinct.

This was what sent me scurrying back home. I had the thought that maybe things were getting worse over time, that the darkness was spilling out from inside the buildings in slow motion, and if I spent too long out in the open it might burst out and overtake me.

But a glance in the antique store proved that wrong. It looked the same as it had. It was distance, not time, that was changing things.

Distance from my house.

From me.

I didn't check any of the houses on my side of the street. I think I didn't want to know if they contained the same darkness, if the unknown lurked just on the other side of my own walls.

In fact, I didn't want to look at them. My own house looked fine. Perfect. Well, not perfect, but perfectly safe. Perfectly real. Every time I thought about looking at the buildings around it, the ones on its side of the street, something welled up inside me, some kind of primal terror, and I forgot how to breathe.

So I didn't look.

It was only after I was back inside my house and thinking about what I'd observed that it hit me: what I could see in the windows was what could be seen from my own. The things in the antique store window might not have existed past the point that was visible from my house. The houses that were too far down the street for there to be a line of sight between my windows and theirs were the weird, blank ones.

What if it wasn't darkness I saw behind the panes, but nothing?

Nothingness?

Nonexistence?

What if the world outside my windows didn't exist, outside of my windows?

Once I had this thought, I knew it was impossible and I knew it was true. This was what freaked me out about being outdoors. When I was inside, there was nothing I could see that couldn't be seen from inside my house, by definition. So everything looked right.

As soon as I was outside, my vantage point changed enough that things were missing. Small things. Distant things. Things at the ends of the street. Probably I was seeing things that weren't there, that I *knew* weren't there, that would be obviously missing if I tried to look at them clearly.

The human brain has a marvelous ability to fill in missing details, if it knows enough about what to expect. You can make out the letters on a sign from farther away if you already know what it says. You can see color out of the corner of your eye, even though that's physically impossible, if your brain knows what color you're supposed to be seeing.

You have a blind spot in both eyes where the optical nerve connects to the retina, but you never notice it. Your brain extrapolates and infers and fills the space with something useful.

What did my side of the street look like, outside of my own townhouse? I knew *its* exterior was fine. I'd looked at it. Maybe as ground zero for... whatever... it played by different rules. Maybe a thing could be seen if it could be seen from any part of the house. I couldn't say. I didn't know the rules. I still don't.

I also don't know what my side of the street looks like, still. I've been outside a few times. Several times, actually. I never look, not even accidentally. My gaze never happens to fall on it. It's like the way you never look at the sun by accident.

I was there for the solar eclipse, not the full one, not where I lived, but a good 85 percent of it, and that was one of the things that surprised me about it: how easy it was to locate the sun in the sky without quite looking at it, how easy it was to stop turning my gaze just short of the point where I would see it and nothing else, before I slipped on my protective glasses.

My entire side of the street was like that. I looked away, without thinking and without trying.

Maybe I could look at it, but I didn't want to. I wasn't sure I could come back from that. It felt like that would be crossing over some threshold, an event horizon from which there could be no coming back. Not if I saw what it looked like, if I saw that much nothingness in living color, not on the other side of a pane of glass but right the fuck there, right next to where I lived...

I never look. I can't look. Or maybe I could, but I don't. That last one is the truth, probably, but it sounds fake.

I take my walks on the other side of the street, eyes carefully tilted to the left or right of me, whatever is towards the buildings and away from the street. The farther I go in either direction, the more I tip my gaze to the side. Looking down the street starts to feel like looking across it. But then I hit a point and it's not safe to look at the buildings, either.

I run out of space and things to look at and there's nowhere I can point my eyes except back along the way I came, and it gets hard to think and hard to breathe until I give up, give in, and go back home.

That is the point past which I cannot go, past which I dare not go. A threshold I cannot cross, for fear of what will happen to me when I do. What I will find. Where I will go.

Even so, I have explored the world I can see from my windows as much as I can, to try to find the shape of this thing, learn some parameters. I've done the same inside.

After weeks of never running out of milk but never quite noticing when more is added, I started marking the level in the jug with a line. It steadily went down with my usage over the course of several days, and then when it was empty I rinsed it, dried it, and then took it out to the recycling can.

When I came back inside, I checked the fridge. The milk was gone. Maybe I'd killed the magic, I thought. Maybe questioning the process had led to a punishment.

Maybe, I even thought, maybe I had somehow been wrong, been utterly mistaken, completely unmoored from any sense of reality and time and only imagined that the jug was lasting any longer than ever. Maybe by keeping track of how much I used, I'd simply grounded myself.

I could almost believe that, but not so much that I felt like going outside and taking a look at the house next to mine. I knew that things were weird. I knew that things were wrong.

Well... I could live without milk, if I had to, but I didn't feel like doing any more experiments that might endanger my supplies of anything else. Even when I woke up the next morning and found a fresh jug of milk in my fridge, I didn't dare doing any further tests. Since the milk had appeared after I resolved not to pry into the hows and whys, it was possible... just possible... that it had been put back in response to that decision. A reward for being good.

That would mean that someone or something was reading my thoughts, probably, unless I'd happened to say it out loud without noticing (this was happening more and more), in which case someone or something was listening.

Was that impossible? No more impossible than anything else, and possibly less.

It took a few days with the new milk jug for me to even get up the nerve to look at it closely, and when I did, I found it had an expiration date: JAN 10.

That was months away. It was September.

Out of curiosity, I picked up one of the individual yogurt cups that were scattered around the top shelf and turned it around in my hands until I found its date: January 10th.

I found another one. Also January 10th.

And another.

The same.

Everything in my fridge, in fact, expired on the 10th of January.

I had two associations for January 10th.

The first one in terms of my personal chronology was that it was my own birthday. January 10th was the very first date I'd ever been aware of, before the Fourth of July or any other date. I learned that dates existed in the process of learning that my birthday was January 10th.

I knew about days before that, and holidays. I'm pretty sure I knew Christmas was a thing before I knew that my birthday had a date.

The second one was a date from history class, which had stuck with me more than most because it fell on my birthday. January 10th was the day that Julius Caesar had led his legion across the Rubicon, the river that marked the boundary of Rome. This action exceeded his legal authority, committing him to either become the absolute ruler of Rome or be executed as a traitor to it.

Victory or death.

The point of no return.

All the food in my fridge expired on January 10th. All the food in my cupboards did, too, including the canned goods that should have been viable for much longer.

I wondered at what point that had happened. It wasn't just stuff that I had been using and that might have been replaced since all of this... whatever this was... had started. Had the fateful date preceded the rest of the weirdness? Had it only happened when I started messing with the milk? Or had it unspooled gradually, unnoticed by me?

There was no way to know now. However it happened, whenever it happened, it had happened. I felt like I'd been given a deadline. For what, I wasn't sure.

Maybe something would happen on January 10th. Maybe that was just when the food would run out. Maybe it was when I would.

Maybe it was my expiration date.

It was September 27th. I had three days, then three months, and then ten more days to go, assuming time wasn't completely out of joint.

I really didn't want to mess with anything else in the house, in case I had somehow triggered the countdown as a punishment by trying to experiment with the parameters of whatever it was I was caught up in. There wasn't anything new to see or do outside, and it hardly seemed worth the oppressive feeling of mounting terror that rose up when I approached the edges of my visible universe just to take a stroll around what passed for a block.

So I spent the dying days of September holed up in the house, reading. Re-reading, actually. I still had a sizable pile of new books to be read, but when I was stressed I found it hard to concentrate on taking in new things, and comforting to revisit old familiar favorites. I was a fast reader anyway, and I always read faster when I was going back over a book I knew and loved. In those three days, I read Terry Pratchett, Ursula Le Guin, Catherynne M. Valente, N.K. Jemisin, and Sunny Moraine.

My library was an unused bedroom that wasn't technically a bedroom because it didn't have a window. That was the other reason I passed the time reading. The view from the windows didn't look wrong, didn't feel wrong, but seeing the world outside had started to remind me of going outside.

If I hadn't been in the library the day after September 30th, I might not have thought to change the calendar over. I had a paper calendar on the wall. Castles of Ireland. It had been a Christmas gift from a distant friend... the only kind I had, really. I didn't have much use for an analog calendar, but since I was seeing it every day it had occurred to me that, being on a deadline, it might be useful to keep track of the passage of time, just in case something happened in the intervening months and I lost the ability to check it electronically. The internet had already gone out by this point, though my computer still worked.

So I flipped the page on the calendar, moving from September to October... or I would have, except the next page was labeled January.

I checked the next month. It was also January. And so were the two after that. I paged back to what had been September, and it was now January, also.

I had a whole year of Januaries, and wouldn't you know it, but every single one of them had a tenth somewhere in it. Waiting.

Someone is dicking with me, I thought. Someone is directing this.

That had to be it. I could say that this is impossible, that everything that's been happening to me is impossible, but since it's all clearly happened there would be no point.

It has happened, and it has happened in a way that can only be deliberate. Deliberate action requires intent, intent requires a mind.

Someone was dicking with me. Someone was jerking me around.

I kind of broke down after my discovery with the calendar, and then I spent a little while just screaming, ranting at the heavens or the unseen lurking force or the people listening in on microphones, whoever or whatever might have been listening. I don't remember everything I said. I'm sure it made sense at the time.

Like I said, I kind of broke down.

Two days past before I formed an intention of my own. I reached it through careful deliberation, after the desperation subsided somewhat.

I decided to proceed as though things made sense, as though there were some logic to it.

January did not follow September in the ordinary course of things. In no practical sense could it actually be January, in the world outside. If there was a world outside. The date of January 10th could hardly have been random, but whatever it related to, it wasn't the actual date.

So I accepted it as a premise that the time was symbolic. It wasn't really January. Maybe it wasn't really any time. The date January 10th was meant to tell me something, and the calendar, too.

I didn't think it was trying to wish me a happy birthday.

So that left the other thing.

The Rubicon.

The threshold.

The point of no return, the point at which you were committed. No takebacks, no second chances, no refunds.

I knew what my Rubicon was.

There was a point past which I dared not go, past which I could not bring myself to even cast my gaze. That didn't mean I couldn't cross it, though. Even if it was physically impossible to look... and I wasn't sure that it was, any more than it would be physically impossible to look at the sun... I could turn around and walk backwards. I could close my eyes and walk slowly onward. I could do it. I could cross it.

What would happen if I did that?

Would I be stepping into nothingness? If so, would that mean I'd cease to exist? Or worse, be trapped nowhere, with no way of getting back to even the bounded existence I had in this non-place?

My life here wasn't so bad. I had everything I needed, except human contact... and I'd basically got by without a lot of that. How long had I been outside the world? How long had I been drifting to get there? How long had it taken me to notice?

I couldn't travel, though. I couldn't do anything new. If I ever tackled my to-be-read pile, I'd never have anything else new to read. There was nothing to watch that I didn't already have. Nothing to see that couldn't be seen from my house.

And things had changed already, degraded. I'd lost the internet. My arrival at my current state of affairs had happened gradually, the change unnoticed by me at first. I couldn't say for sure that it wouldn't keep changing.

I'd take the risk, I decided. I could do nothing else.

Once I made up my mind, it didn't seem worth it to wait. I could cross the days off one by one until I reached January 10th, but I'd already decided the date was symbolic. It wasn't really January, if it was really any time. It wouldn't be the 10th in a week. There was no countdown because it was a message, not a deadline.

If I was wrong, I could be walking into oblivion... but if I was right, I could still be walking into oblivion. I had no true knowledge of the nature of my environment and no control over anything except myself. It was possible that what the action I was contemplating was just impossible, that it wouldn't work, that I would remain trapped.

If that happened, I would revise my assumptions. Keep counting the days until the calendar said it was January 10th, and then see what, if anything, happened. If nothing did, or nothing that prevented me from moving outside the house, I would try again. Just in case I was partly right.

So, now, I have a plan, and I have a backup plan. Somehow the backup plan makes me feel better about the uncertainty of the plan.

I'm not taking any supplies. Maybe that seems foolish, but I can't imagine that it will matter. I can't explain why. What I kind of hope will happen is that I close my eyes, move past the point of no return, and open them to find out that I'm just... back in the world. Back in my life. Back in normal space and time, whatever that means. If that's the case, I can just turn around walk home.

But maybe I'll find myself somewhere else. Maybe I'll be even further removed from the existence I knew. I don't know. But I can't imagine how a backpack full of canned peaches and spare batteries would help me. I don't think it's that kind of situation. I don't think I'm in that kind of story.

This is the Rubicon. The point of no return. The point of full commitment. When I cross over, if I can cross over... it'll be do or die. Either I'll be free, gone from here... or else just gone.

There's no hedging this bet and no doing it halfway.

Alea iacta est.

Going Sideways

Angel found me behind my trailer after our last show in Des Moines, the last of our run in Iowa.

Normally we would have pulled up stakes literally as well as figuratively already, but there was a slight hitch with the contract for our next venue and the show wasn't going to get on the road towards a spot a couple hundred miles away without a firm deal. The only thing worse than being stuck in one place was being stuck in between them.

We had the lot until midnight, officially, and the owner probably wouldn't come by to run us off until the morning.

I didn't like being stuck in one place any more than anyone else in the show did, didn't like the uncertainty. It was always lean times for a traveling show, and the arc of the universe was that it just kept on getting leaner. We all knew how shows like ours died: suddenly. Keeping a show on the road was a bit like keeping a bunch of bowling pins in the air. No, not bowling pins. Knives and torches. As long as everything kept moving and the juggler never missed a beat, it looked so fluid, so natural.

But one mistake would be too many.

One missed trick could bring the whole thing a-tumbling down.

Back at the end of the golden ages of circuses, whenever a show closed down one of the big boys would send scouts to pick through the remains, hiring away talent and buying whatever was worth having at a fire sale price. Eventually, inevitably, all the biggest boys had wound up eating each other, creating a multi-headed, tentacled monstrosity called Ringling Brothers Barnum and Bailey Circus, but now even that was gone. The golden age was so long gone even the ghosts had moved on. If our show died, our stock would just sit there until it was impounded and then be sold at auction. No scouts were waiting in the wings to scoop up the survivors.

The best of us might wind up on a TV talent show in five years, hoping for one last shot at glory. The rest would never see a spotlight again.

I knew a lot of people who had left the life. Left? I guess it would be more accurate to say they'd lost it. Lost it, and never found anything better. The number of folks I knew who had truly moved on, gotten jobs in the straight world... that I could count on one hand.

Most of us dealt with it by not dealing with it, always focusing on what needs doing and then on the next thing. The next act, the next show, the next big trick. Some said we had to compete with YouTube and Netflix and video games, but I never saw it that way. Nothing we could do would compete with the digital media.

But the flip side was that nothing they could do would compare with what we did, which was art. Artifice and artistry. We were craftsmen and we were confidence tricksters, and everything we did was art, in every sense of the word. We never stopped working on it because that was who we were, and because that was what amounted to an accomplishment in this life. That was how you won the game, at least for a while.

No one got rich in a traveling show.

No one really made it, not anymore.

That's what we were: a traveling show. "Circus" and "carnival" both had both specific meanings and connotations it was useful to avoid, when booking a venue and securing a license, so we were never anything more specific than a show on the paperwork. Our manager would use words like "variety show", "athletic exhibition", and "performance art", depending on where he was and who he was talking to.

I was working on my own next big thing when Angel found me, though my heart wasn't really in it. My mind wasn't on it. I kept thinking about another trick, something sensational, something truly new, something no one else could do, but which I couldn't do on my own. That was when she showed up, exactly as if my thoughts had summoned her.

I'd been trying to catch her eye for two days of the three-day engagement, been trying to steal a moment alone with her for a private conversation. I'd almost managed it once, the first time, because her guard wasn't up. As soon as she found out what I wanted to talk about, though, she'd ghosted me so hard she might as well have disappeared every time she wasn't on stage.

In point of fact, I wasn't entirely sure she hadn't done that.

"Angel," I said. "Hey. I was just thinking about you."

Her eyes flicked over to the wooden stand-up figure, which had two of my knives sticking out of it.

"I'll try not to take that personally," she said. "I always thought the idea was to *not* hit the volunteer."

"That is the general idea, yes," I said. "But I'm always up for trying something new. In fact, I've been hoping to talk to you about it."

"I had a feeling you might be," she said. "But... it wasn't the right time. Not in the middle of a run."

"You know, I agree," I said. "But now that we've got some time..."

"My thought exactly," she said.

"Do you want to go somewhere?" I asked. I didn't want to suggest my trailer, or hers. Both of those somehow seemed to be worse ideas than the other. But I didn't think she wanted this to be a public conversation.

"How about the main hall?" she asked. The fairgrounds we'd rented had a great big corrugated metal barn of a building that we'd used in lieu of setting of up our own marquee. One of the many differences from yesteryear. The first time I'd seen Barnum & Bailey as a kid had been inside a civic center. I'd grown up in the life and had never even seen a proper big top.

"That's private enough for you?" I asked her.

"No one's in there," she said. "No one has any reason to be in there. I told Marty I need the space to plot out something new, so he let me have the key."

"Okay. Lead the way."

We wound our way through the field. All the marquees and stands had been taken down. Even with the standing exhibition hall and the outbuildings, we'd still had a few tents of our own. It was less that the show was big enough to require them and more that it was helpful if the show looked big. Nothing draws a crowd like a crowd, so of course it helped to crowd the field up a bit in advance. Create avenues and alleys out of a wide-open space. That sort of thing.

Like I said: artifice and artistry.

The hangar-like building was closed up and padlocked, but Angel had a key on a stretchy wristband. She left the main doors closed and instead opened up a regular-sized door on the side of the building, then took me by the wrist and twirled sideways through it, pulling me through and shutting the door behind us like she suddenly had a fear of being spotted with me.

"Whoa," I said, regaining my balance after a sudden burst of vertigo. My eyes were adjusting to the murky blue lighting inside, after the harsh orange sodium glow of the stadium-style lights outside. I hadn't been in this hall at night with the main lights off. The emergency lighting situation was kind of creepy. "Look at the state of this place."

I was a little surprised to see the folding chairs still sitting in the rows we'd put them in three days before. They belonged to the venue, but I was sure there had to be something in the contract about putting them away. The floor looked filthy, too. Smudgy and gross. We very rarely left a place in a better state than we found it, but there was natural wear and tear and then there was burning bridges.

Even if we weren't required to clean up, I knew Marty didn't like to leave behind the posters and buntings. He'd reuse them until they were in tatters. Had to. We certainly couldn't afford to leave behind the sound equipment and lighting that were still in position, or any of the props that were lying around.

Enough was wrong with the whole picture that if I hadn't seen the tents come down outside, I would have wondered if we weren't booked for an extended engagement. Our crew could break down a stage pretty damn quickly if they had a mind to, but there was no reason to wait for the last minute. Hell, usually the first minute was the last one. It was only an outside circumstance that had kept us on the spot, and we'd need to move as soon as that was resolved, since we'd be behind schedule.

It was almost enough to make me forget about Angel and go find Martin. Again, if I hadn't seen the crew at work, I would have been having visions of roustabouts drinking themselves into a stupor over the unscheduled delay. The crew was up and at it, and yet...

"Do you know what's going on here?" I said, waving my hand around at the clutter. "I know you said Martin said you can have the hall, but did he know it hadn't been cleared out yet?"

"You don't have to worry about that," she said. "It's really not as bad as it looks from here. Please, Tony. I wanted to talk to you about what you thought you saw, on opening night."

That was enough to make me forget about the state of the hall.

"What I saw," I said. "I know I saw it. Don't... don't patronize me, okay? I don't know what I saw, exactly, but I know I saw it, and I hope you can explain it better than I can."

"It's just, I've been working on a new trick with Bartholdi and it's not ready yet..."

"That was no trick," I said. "And you weren't working. I've never known anyone who is as good at what she does as you are, who works less at it. There's a change that comes over you when you finish a set. I've seen it. Most of us only get it when we wrap up a run, or even the season, but you clock out as soon as you're done. The show was over and you were clocked out, mentally. I don't think I've ever seen you more relaxed."

"That's true," she said. "I was relaxed... too relaxed. I was careless. I should never have let you see it."

"So now we get at the truth," I said. "Angel, I'm your friend! I can't believe you tried to lie to me!"

"Because friend or not, it was none of your business," she said. "And because it's my safety that's at stake, not yours."

That stung.

"Don't you trust me?" I said. "Because I trust you. I'd trust you with anything."

"Then trust me with the decision of what I can safely tell you," she said. "If I told you that this is my life and I need you to not ask any more questions, not bring it up again, not mention it to me or anyone else... just not say another word about it, would you? Would you do that for me?"

"I mean... could we talk about it first?" I said. "I think I'd have an easier time promising not to ask any questions in the future if I had the answers already, don't you?"

"I can see why you'd think that," she said. "This is your first time going through this, but I've seen the other side of it time and time again. Believe me, it doesn't help. Talking it out... some hungers only grow when you feed them. It's better if I don't indulge your..."

"Natural curiosity?"

"I was going to say entitlement," she said.

"Look, I don't feel *entitled*," I said. "Just curious. How could I not be curious? Who wouldn't be? I've got questions... and yes, I would prefer if you answered them. I don't think that's entitlement. I don't think you owe me them. I don't think you owe me anything. I just think it would be better if you answered them."

"Better for whom? For you?"

"Well, and for you," I said. "I mean, if your ideal is that I never talk about it again."

"That feels an awful lot like blackmail."

"For the love of God, Angel, stop reading into my intentions!" I said. "We're both on the same side here. If you want to drop it forever, then that's what I want to do. If you don't want to answer my questions first, I can't make you. But you told me you think it'll be easier that way, and I happen to disagree. There's nothing selfish or entitled about that. We both want the same thing here. I'm just offering a different perspective on how we get there."

She looked at me, and it was hard to read the expression on her face, but it definitely wasn't a happy one.

"Okay, Tony," she said. "Let me try it your way. But you promise that if I do this, if I do it your way, if we have this conversation, then you'll let it drop? Forever? No more questions, no sly allusions, no references to a shared secret, no talking about how you're not talking about it?"

"Jesus, Angel, what do you take me for?" I asked.

"I told you, this isn't my first time going around like this," she said.

"I swear, I will act like I never saw anything and that this conversation never happened. I just have to be satisfied within my own head and then I'll, you know, file it away on a back shelf. But if I'm not satisfied... I mean, as a performer I can school my face pretty well, but I'd be thinking about it every time I saw you, and I don't think I could keep from acting like there's a big mystery. Not all the time. But I can keep a secret, I promise you that."

"Okay," she said. "Just remember that it's my secret you'll be keeping. What do you want to know?"

"The big question first: how do you do it?"

"If you're asking about the physics or metaphysics of it, I couldn't tell you," she said. "I've had theories, I guess you could call them, but they're more like... fantasies. Like I was a faerie changeling who grew up. Or an alien princess. Or a mutant superhero. I'd make up explanations for where I go..."

"So you don't just disappear?" I asked. "I mean, you're not invisible, you're... really gone?"

"Yes, I'm gone," she said. "I can step out of the world at one place, and step back into it again, in the same place, or a different one. That's what I do."

"Okay, so, forget 'how' in the bigger sense," I said. "How did you learn to do it? Figure out you could?"

"I've always been able to do it. As long as I can remember, maybe even longer. My mother had so many stories about me getting out of my crib, past the baby gate, into places I wasn't supposed to be. I don't know if that wasn't just normal baby stuff, though. When I was a little bit older, when I was a toddler, I guess I figured out that I wasn't supposed to do it long before I worked out that other people couldn't. My mother would yell at me to never do that again, stay close, never get out of her sight. Stuff like that."

"She yelled at you?"

"Fear, not anger," she said. "For all the difference it makes to a child. But, I mean, I get it now. Your baby is there and you turn to look at a sign and you turn back and she's gone, nowhere in sight. Missing in a crowd, or on an empty street... I'm not sure which is scarier, to be honest. I didn't understand

85

why she was upset with me, only that she was. Again, I don't think it's substantially different from normal kid stuff, from her point of view. I think most parents have a scare or two like that. Honestly, there have been times when I heard parents talking about their kids that I wondered if we don't all start out like this and then grow out of it. But I've worked the crowds enough times to see kids just toddle aggressively away from their parents in a moment of distraction. Lightning in a diaper. Anyway, I didn't know why it distressed my mom, only that it did, and so I stopped doing it."

"How long did that last?"

"Until I hit the double digits, or thereabouts," she said. "By that point I had figured out that other people can't just... do what I do."

"Do you have to talk around it like that?" I asked. "It kind of sounds like you're ashamed."

"I don't really know what to call it," she said. "I don't usually talk about it. I don't have the words for it. What would you call it?"

"Vanishing? Teleportation?"

"From my point of view, I'm not vanishing," she said. "I just... leave the place I'm in. Like exiting a room. And I don't know about teleporting."

"It means..."

"I know what it means," she said. "I just don't know if it applies. I think there's some baggage with that word that might lead to a false impression, while at the same time it doesn't really convey the totality of the experience. I don't think it's the right word. I don't have the right word but I don't think that's what it is. I think of it as side-stepping, but of course that doesn't mean the right thing to anyone else."

"Okay," I said. "The thing I don't understand... I mean, I don't understand any of it, but the thing that maybe you can illuminate, is what does Bartholdi have to do with it? Obviously you don't need him. He wasn't even on the grounds when I saw you vanish, and from what you say, you were doing it for years before you knew him. So why is he part of the act?"

"Technically, I'm part of his act," she said. "It's Bartholdi the Magnificent and his beautiful assistant, remember?"

"But, I mean, *why*?" I said. "Why isn't it your act? Why is Bartholdi the magician and not you?

"Because I'm his beautiful assistant," she said.

"He should be your assistant!"

"Are you saying he's more beautiful than me?" she asked.

"Listen, you're more than qualified for that position, but I think you've got him beat for the other one, too," I said. "What you can do..."

"What can I do?" she said.

"I watched you vanish into thin air!"

"That's what we do," she said. "The magician waves his hands and says the magic words. The lady... vanishes. That's it. That's the act."

"But it's his name on the posters! It should be yours!"

"Why would it be?"

"Because you're the one with the magic!" I said. "*He's* the talent? You're the one with the talent! He's a fraud, he's riding your coattails! He's taking advantage of you!"

"What do you think most magicians are doing, when their assistants step inside the box of mysteries?" she said. "Who do you think does the heavy lifting on any trick, the one who's out of sight, or the one who is standing in the spotlight, waving their hands for the rubes? For any gag we do that relies on me, he's doing the exact same thing he would be doing if we were playing with false backs, trapdoors, and mirrors. If anything, I'm the one relying on his skills to carry the act."

"You don't mean that!"

"You said it yourself, Tony: I clock out a lot earlier than anyone else in the show does. That's because I just don't work as hard as anyone. I don't have to. Now, there's a thing I can do. I don't know if I do it well and I don't know if I do it poorly. I've just... always been able to do it. Maybe that's a kind of talent, I don't know. But I'm no magician. That's skill, that's stagecraft, that's presence. Bartholdi, he can... he knows how to do things. He can reach out to the crowd and grab them. He can hold their attention in the palm of his hand. I don't know if you've noticed, but he has a lot more going on than just disappearing acts."

"But that's the grand finale," I said.

"Because he has to work up to it," she said. "Otherwise... I mean, you know what an anti-climax is? Like a shaggy dog story, you build and you build and you just keep building things up and then it never goes anywhere. Just fizzles out, trails off. Anti-climax."

"There's nothing anti-climactic about what you can do," I said.

"Right. I've got the opposite problem. Do you know why Bartholdi closes the show?"

"Because he's the headliner," I said.

"Okay, back it up. Why does the headliner close the show? Why not have the best act on first?"

"Someone needs to warm up the crowd."

"Could anyone do that better than the biggest crowd-pleaser on the ticket? Come on. What's the real reason you have to have the biggest act go on last?"

"...because no one wants to follow them."

"Because no one wants to follow them," she said. "You can't start with a big trick because then you've got nowhere to go but down. And me... I've got nowhere to go. I'm a one trick pony."

"It's a hell of a trick!" I said.

"Is it?" she said. "Listen, I tried doing a couple of solo acts, before I hooked up with Bartholdi. They didn't exactly bring the house down. The thing is... the thing is... if you see what I can do, if you really see it, there's no trick to it. No trick at all. I only ever did it twice that way. Both times, it went the same way. I started by showing the audience what I could do: now you see me, now you don't. Disappear at one end of the stage, but in plain sight and with no flash or smoke or screen, and reappear at the other end. That wasn't supposed to be the whole act, but it's as far as I ever got."

"Why? What happened?"

"First came the screams. Everybody's expecting something but no one expects to see... what they see. And these were small crowds, in small venues. They were close. Some of them were just sort of letting out a shout because they're startled, but some of the screams were the real deal. Deep-seated terror. Real deep-seated, real terror. Because they know what they've seen is wrong, they know it's impossible. And then after the screams comes the silence. Dead silence, the worst sound a performer can ever hear. It's not like a hush. A hush is just the world holding its breath. It's still there. Dead silence. Dead room. And then, someone laughed. One person laughed, and it cut through the silence, and then other people laugh, because it's stupid, it's *so* stupid, obviously it was fake, what kind of a ridiculous gag was I trying to pull?"

"But it's not a gag, it's real!"

"But it *can't* be real, which means it *must* be fake," she said. She waved a hand at Bartholdi's props, the guillotine and the coffin and the box propped up on the sawhorses. "All of this *could* be fake, which is enough to relax and accept it as real."

"That doesn't make any sense."

"Yeah? That's magic for you," she said. "That's show biz. The second time, I had... a bad moment. During the silence. I was glad when the laughter started, I was relieved, because I thought it was going to be pitches and torchforks. Torches and... you know what I mean. That's how I figured out my act works a lot better if I was out of sight. Behind a curtain, inside a box, locked in a trunk. Only... well, I didn't have the most stage presence before. When I wasn't even present on the stage, it only got worse."

"But if you're hidden away, your act isn't any different from any other disappearing act," I said.

"Well, I mean, it's easier," she said. "Some people train their whole lives to get out of safes and water tanks."

"Yeah, but... oh, that's it!" I said. "Escapology! You shouldn't be doing magic. You're an escape artist! You don't need Bartholdi waving his hands and reciting fake Egyptian incantations to pretend he's transporting you through the nether realm. You just need a barker, an announcer, like an emcee, someone with the patter to keep the audience engaged, lay out all the dangers you're in and the death you're defying. You could be a star!"

"That would be cheating," she said.

"How is it... it's the same gags you do as a magician's assistant," I said.

"Like I said: some people train their whole lives to do that," she said. "And they're recognized for their skill. Magic is... magic. Everyone expects it to be fake, and if you accept it's real... I mean, what I do, it might as well be magic. It might *be* magic. It doesn't feel dishonest. I can't bill myself as an escape artist. Anyway, this is the information age. If I'm getting myself out of a time-locked vault or a car that's been buried in cement, someone's going to want to know how it's done. With magic, everyone accepts that it's a trick and moves on. There's a reason we don't do anything that hasn't been done before. None of the hardcore illusion geeks has to wonder how we do it, so none of them pull the string and pick it apart."

"So you can do something that no one else on earth can do, but you won't use it except to do things that anyone could do?"

"Look, I'm just happy I figured out a way that I can actually use my 'talent' all the time and get paid for it," she said. "Legally, I mean. I'm in show biz. It's not glamorous but it's what I dreamed about. You know the dream, I know you know it. And it's so easy, for me. I step into a box. I step out of a box. The boxes change, but it's always the same gag. I make my money, I have enough free time to read. And I'm the only person who can always find a quiet moment in the middle of a show. I just... step away."

"What's it like?"

"It's... peaceful," she said. "It's not like you think it is, not teleportation like in the movies. I just sort of... step sideways. Out of the box. Out of the world. It's honestly easier when I'm locked inside something, because then I can be sure I'm stepping the *right kind* of sideways. Sometimes I still get forget."

"So you step from one place to another? From one side of the stage to another? Out of the box and into your trailer?"

"No, I told you, it's not like that," she said. "I don't just blip out somewhere and blip in somewhere else. I can vanish in the blink of an eye, but it's not instantaneous transportation. I can't use it to see the world, or even pop downtown to buy a loaf of bread. I just step a little bit outside of the world. And then I can walk around, the same as normal. Just like you're doing right now."

"What's it look like, the other world?"

"Like this," she said, gesturing around. "It's not really another world, you know. It's just the outside of the one you know. Things that have been sitting in one place long enough become real on the other side. Things that haven't just sort of leave a faint impression. A smudge. A ghost. A hint. They become more solid the longer they sit. I think of it as leaving a crease in the fabric of reality. It's tricky to get around when we're new in town and just setting up, because nothing we bring with us looks real, but by the time we open enough of our stuff is there for me to orient myself. Bartholdi always lays the tape down for our spots as soon as we get into town, so that even if the box isn't there on the other side, I can see where it is when I need to step back into it.

"Can you take other people with you?"

"...yes," she said.

"You sound unsure about that. Have you ever actually tried?"

"I've done it," she said. "I mean, I've had to do it. Sometimes. It's not something I enjoy, or like thinking about."

"Had to?"

"I don't like it," she said. "It wasn't my idea, the first time, and it's never my first choice. But sometimes... someone finds out what I can do, and can't be persuaded that they're mistaken, and they want to expose me, or they won't give up the idea that I could be doing something better, could be doing something more. When that happens... I mean, I know how it goes. First there's excitement, and then frustration, and then anger."

"Does showing them help, somehow?" I asked. "Because I'd be willing to see."

"I'm not talking about just showing them," she said. "I'm talking about leaving them. A one-way trip."

She hugged herself, looking away. I shivered. That sounded like murder, very slow murder... and yet also the perfect crime. Nobody would ever find the body.

"Well, I'm glad you decided to talk to me instead," I said. "But that's why you were afraid to? Don't worry, it won't come to that. I won't be like that, I swear! Honestly, I'm only looking to help you here."

"Oh, yes," she said. "That comes right before the frustration: the righteousness. You're only thinking of me."

"I am!" I said. "I mean it!"

"I know you do," she said. "Tony, at the start of this, you said if I answered your questions, you'd let it drop. Do you have any more questions for me?"

"Just... how can you be happy, playing second banana? You can do something no one else can do!"

"I don't know that," she said. "You don't know that. Maybe the world is full of beautiful assistants who all came to the same conclusion I did. Maybe the only reason you haven't heard of anyone else who can do what I do is because it never works out for anyone who tries to do anything flashy with it. If all the rest of your questions are about how I can make a particular decision, the answer to all of them is: it's my life. That's all the answer you need."

"The hell it is!"

"It's all the answer you're getting," she said. "And more answer than you're entitled to. Tony, you told me that if I answered your questions, you'd be satisfied."

"Well, I didn't think your answers would be so unsatisfying."

"And I warned you that they would be," she said. "Are you going to keep your word, or not? I really need to know."

"Of course," I said. "Angel, you should know by now that I'm honest. I say what I mean. I mean what I say. I said I wouldn't bring it up again, and I won't. But..."

"...but what?"

"But you could change your mind about that," I said.

"Are you going to try to change it?"

"I mean, it's up to you," I said. "No matter what I say or do, it's still up to you. It's not like I can actually force you to change your mind. And I promised I wouldn't talk about it, and I meant it, and I'm going to keep my promise..."

"But now you're thinking that you never promised not to talk to me about the promise itself," she said. "Because if you can get me to change my mind about that, then you can talk to me about the rest of it. You really were thinking of me when you threw your knives at the target, weren't you?"

"Not to hit you!" I said. "And I mean, it would be a hell of an act. You'd get your name on the posters for sure."

"The daring Fortunato and his beautiful assistant, Angel?"

"It's just one idea!" I protested. "One idea for how you could use your, your gift, in the spotlight. Even if we did a double act, you would have first billing. Angel and Fortunato. You'd deserve it."

"So you'd be my assistant?"

"I don't think we have to define things in a hierarchy," I said. "We'd both bring something to the table. I just think your talents merit the top spot"

"Because however we bill it, you think you'd get Bartholdi's spot at the top of the card?" she said.

"It's not about me taking his spot," I said. "It's about helping you claim it for yourself. Can't you see, I don't want to steal you away from Bart? Angel, I want to set you free!"

"I am free," she said. "You don't have to like the choices I make with my freedom, but you have to let me make them. That's what freedom is."

"I just want what's best for you," I said. "I mean that."

"I know you think you do. And that's why I have to leave now."

"Angel, don't go!" I said.

"Goodbye, Tony," she said, and then... the lady vanished.

Maybe it was my imagination or maybe it was because I'd heard her describe it, but I would swear I saw her actually step *sideways*. Not to the left or the right but in some other direction entirely, something I didn't quite have the capacity to sort out when I saw it and definitely didn't have the words to describe.

She was gone without a pop or a shower of sparks or a cloud of smoke, and I had to admit that I sort of saw what she meant. It was a little too real, so real that the mind sort of rebelled. It was like coming face to face with a bit of the supernatural. In the weird sickly blue lighting of the exhibition hall, it was freaky as hell... and "freaky" is not a word I used lightly.

But just because none of the obvious uses would work didn't mean she had to spend out her days playing second fiddle to a drunken fraud like "Bartholdi". Stagecraft? Showmanship? She didn't need him, and I was sure I could prove it. I'd figure out what she could do with her gift and then she'd be free.

It seemed obvious to me that she wanted that. I figured that's why she had left me, instead of taking me with her and stranding me in that weird alternate dimension, the way she had the others, the ones who wouldn't keep their word and who had tried to browbeat her into seeing things their way.

That was a horrible thing to think about, being trapped forever in a shadow dimension... or maybe not forever, maybe just however long it took to waste away. I doubted you could eat an impression of food, to say nothing of the state it would be in after standing still long enough to show up. It would probably be just about as appetizing as the dingy puffs of popcorn that had accumulated in the seams along the bottoms of the walls over the course of our three-day run.

I pushed the thought from my head and headed out of the hall. The door was still unlocked, but I didn't have the key to lock it behind me. Well, that would be on Angel, if anything happened. Not that there was anyone on the lot who wasn't family... though, I noticed there didn't seem to be anyone around at the moment.

The light outside was as sickly blue as it had been inside the hall. It was dim, too. Not dark like the night, not lit like the lighting, but just dim, uniformly dim everywhere. I looked up to see where it was coming from and the sky was a blurry mess of fuzzy lines, like a time lapse photo of the sky viewed through cloudy glass.

I could say the truth of my situation hit me like a ton of bricks, but it wasn't even that. It was more ephemeral than that, like the impression of a ton of bricks might have left on the fabric of reality, here on the other side of the canvas wall. The reality didn't feel real to me yet, not really real.

No, the thing that smacked me hard in the face and cut me to the core of my being in the moment of realization was the unfairness of the situation, the gross, monstrous injustice of it all. Knowing that Angel had pulled me through to the other side before I even had a chance to talk to her, and then left me here... that hurt. That really hurt.

Being lumped in with those other guys, the ones who had been pushy, who'd tried to take advantage, the ones who'd had no respect for her wishes and no regard for her safety...

Though now that I thought about it, I realized I only had her word on that, I'd only heard her version of events. Who was to say any of them were any more guilty than I was? She'd prejudged me from the start, I realized. I had been perfectly civil, honest and forthright with her even when she made it clear she felt no obligation to be truthful with me. It obviously didn't matter what I'd actually said or done, which meant she'd made her mind up about me from the beginning.

I was damned, trapped and doomed to die in a shadow world because of Angel's trust issues. If I could have convinced myself I deserved it, I think maybe I could have accepted my fate with grace. But I was too honest to lie to myself and too self-aware to believe it if I tried.

The fact was, there wasn't a single thing I could have done differently to save myself, and I knew it.

To think that I might live out the rest of my life with that knowledge, die with that knowledge...

It was all so unconscionably cruel.

Couldn't she understand that I'd only wanted to help her?

Made With Love

When I made Annabelle, I wasn't looking for a companion. I hadn't known at the time how much I needed one.

I never thought of myself as lonely as a child, even though I was frequently alone and didn't have anyone who shared my interests. I was simply solitary. My interests were unique, or so I thought at the time. The adults in my life assured each other I would become interested in boys any time, and then some of them assured me it would be fine if I was interested in girls.

Mostly I was interested in making things, and in the strange blue stone that dotted the quarries and rocky outcroppings near our home, and in making things out of the stone.

Astralite, it was called. The star-stone. People used to think it came to the earth in falling stars, but that's nonsense.

A geologist once told me we have no idea what made astralite form, but it definitely had a terrestrial origin. I don't know that I could have articulated this as a child, but the way it appeared in veins running through the limestone certainly testified to that.

The name had stuck even after its celestial origin was disproven, because it was popular and evocative and it certainly fit in other ways. The luminescent qualities of the star-stone were one of its many notable qualities.

Despite the difficulties involved in commercial exploitation, high-quality astralite has always been in demand. I was fortunate that our local strain was not seen by anyone as particularly pure or interesting. It marbled our limestone with whisker-thin wisps, not great galloping rivers.

Over the course of several summers, I collected slivers and dust and pressed them into molds of my own devising, stamping out the gears and shafts and other bits that would become Annabelle. I'd created the technique to make jewelry that I gave away as gifts.

Astralite has a tricky reputation for jewelry. My mother still has the first pendant I ever made, but everyone has heard about the rich lawyer who had astralite stones faceted and polished like gems set into a necklace for his wife, only for them to break apart completely before she opened the box. The world is full of stories like both of these: the cherished astralite heirloom and the junk jewelry that disintegrates.

Sometimes astralite is solid as the strongest of bedrock. Sometimes it is fragile as hematite, soapstone, or amber. People chalk this up to differences in composition or structure, though no one's been able to reliably measure such differences.

Those who work astralite will tell you the truth, though most people think we're just being romantic.

It's really simple, though.

You have to love it.

The proof of this sits next to me on the sofa every evening, and lays beside me in bed while I sleep. I pressed her parts together out of dust and scrapings, but in twenty-three years not a single piece has broken, not a single axle has cracked. There isn't so much as a chip on the tooth of any of her gears.

People think I'm a genius. Even the ones who believe I'm a fraud — and that's most people — think I'm a genius at it. Even making a person-shaped machine that can walk and speak like a person is something of a holy grail in the field of robotics, an area in which I have no actual expertise or experience.

If Annabelle were nothing more than a remote-controlled automaton and all those intricate visible clockwork pieces suspended inside the thin blue glowing wire frame that bounds her limbs were simply there for show, she would still be a triumph in both design and execution.

The truth is, I don't know how I made her. I started with the simple idea for an astralite clock. The immediate inspiration for this was an old spring-driven alarm clock my parents had, which I had taken apart and put back together many times.

As soon as I started making the pieces, though, I found that they pulled me in a different direction. I started making more pieces, other pieces, and putting them together in the way that made the most sense.

I started when I was eleven. It took three years, during which time most of the adults in my life thought I was making an impressive sculpture. When asked, I only said, "or something like that."

I'd had a vague inkling in my head of what my labor was leading to, but it sounded ridiculous to say it aloud.

I was making a person.

I was making a girl.

I was making a friend.

People tell me she is a work of art. I used to correct them by saying that her creation was done out of love, but I've stopped, mostly because I realized that the two aren't mutually exclusive.

Still, I don't like to hear Annabelle described that way, as a work. "A thing of beauty" is another one that makes me see red, though that one is also applied to other women.

When I was a child, I made Annabelle the size of a child. Since then, I have grown and she has grown with me. She bathes in astralite dust periodically, according to her own unfathomable internal rhythms. She takes it into herself. She grows. She changes.

We are adults now. We live together, loving each other yet not quite lovers, at least not in the sense that my more prurient correspondents assume. They like to ask how we have sex. I used to ask them why they assumed that we do, but more often than not, this would only result in even cruder inquiries in the next follow-up.

I support my love and myself with my astralite art and jewelry, which I sell to a select clientele in order to preserve my reputation for quality. It's not enough for the customer to love a piece in the aesthetic sense, or to love the idea of having it. There has to be real love attached to it, flowing through it.

Astralite needs love to survive when removed from its rocky womb.

That's the secret.

That's the key.

That's why I can work it as easily as if it were soft clay, and make a sculpture you can't dent with a sledgehammer. When my pieces leave me and go out into the world, though, my love for them cannot sustain them. They must go to loving homes. They must be purchased with love, given with love, treasured.

Annabelle helps me vet my clients. While my explanations of astralite's nature are still regarded as new age fringe theories by many, they are known. So are the qualifications I set for buying my pieces. Many have tried to bluff their way through the interview.

Usually it's obvious when someone is faking, covering their covetousness with cartoon hearts in their eyes. I can be fooled, though.

People can even fool themselves.

Annabelle, the treasure of my heart, is never fooled. Love comes as naturally to her as breathing does to you or me. If this means she does not often have to stop and ponder about its existence, it means she acutely notices its absence.

Even with the vetting process, I offer no guarantees with my work, as things can change, and hearts change with them. I've heard from people who received one of my pieces secondhand, often through a bequest or at an estate sale, only to have it fall to pieces. Usually they're just complaining, but in a few cases a new owner has sought my help in establishing that the piece was a counterfeit so they could seek redress from the seller. When this occurs, I have no choice but to disappoint them again.

On the other hand, I've received many kind messages from people who have found a secondhand treasure which appeared pitted and pocked but which cleaned up more nicely than they would have thought possible with a little tender love and care, or who received a cherished keepsake from a family member and want me to know how they feel closer to their loved one than ever when they wear or handle it.

I also receive several inquiries a week asking me for instructions on how to build another Annabelle, along with offers to buy her or requests that I make her available for an in-depth examination. I used to try to respond to these, but now I don't bother.

It's not even the volume of them. It's the fact that even explaining that she is a person whom I love feels like I'm granting too much legitimacy to the premise that she's not. It wears me down.

I couldn't tell someone how to make another one of her. I don't think there could be another one of her, any more than there could be another one of me, or you, or anyone else. I doubt copying her framework or the pattern of her gears would create another spritely blue glowing woman who laughs at my jokes and shares my fears.

The mechanics by which her physical form were constructed hardly matter. That's not what made her. Sometimes, when I receive a query about her origins that is neither presumptive nor insensitive, I share what advice I have to give on the subject, though to my knowledge no one has yet succeeded in making another living person out of astralite, at least not on purpose.

I did receive an email yesterday from a hysterical mother whose daughter had found one of my tiny carved hummingbirds with its wing broken off. The girl had pressed the pieces back together. She wants to be a veterinarian, her mother said, and she cooed over the poor broken thing, and made it a tiny bandage, and kissed it better, and now a tiny blue hummingbirds follows her around, flitting around in circles around her head and watching over her while she sleeps.

Her mother wanted to know if this is normal.

I told her it's natural.

Women Making Bees In Public

She sits at a wrought iron table outside the cafe. The table has six sides, the mesh on top a sturdy hexagonal lace. A cup of tea with honey cools atop a bone saucer, untouched.

She's wearing an extremely well-fitted double-breasted houndstooth jacket of the sort I think you would call a peacoat. Dark gray leggings protrude from beneath it. Her hair is pulled back and up in a high, tight bun, presumably to keep it out of her face while she works.

Spread out on a soft piece of suede unfurled in front of her are a plethora of parts — tiny, delicate, and beautiful. Gold wire legs and antennae, fine-toothed cogs, wings made of leaf so thin you can see through it.

She sews them into place once the jeweled carapace is in position using a needle so small she needs a jeweler's loupe to thread it, then pokes at a spot where the thorax joins the abdomen to set something in motion within.

The new-minted bee starts with a shake, sets its wings to buzzing, streaks in circles beneath the umbrella overhead and zips off.

There are no chairs at her table save the one in which she sits. She has been there every time I've chanced to pass this way, and on the occasions such as today when it wasn't chance at all. I have been here almost since she began, and now that she's finished, I stand, frozen.

What to do now? Every time I've watched her finish before, I've turned and hurried away before I could see what, if anything, she would do next. Pull a book out of her handbag and start reading? Get up and leave?

Except she almost always had her tea, as she does now, untouched.

I watch her watch the bee past the point where I can no longer begin to follow where it's gone. She then smiles to herself. I can almost hear the soft sigh of contentment she lets out. She settles back in her seat.

I want to go up to her, to tell her my name and ask hers. I want to ask her *how* and *why* and a hundred questions, but above all *how*. I want to be her new best friend. I want to do all of this and more, but I can't bring myself to intrude upon this elegant, solitary woman who makes bees on a coffee shop patio.

Not without some sign, some small sign, that she would be receptive...

Too late, I realize that she's looking around and that the sweep of her eyes are on a collision course with mine. Her smile broadens and she says, "Hello."

It is probably a mistake to judge someone's voice based on two syllables projected across a distance in the open air, and had it transpired that her voice was anything other than everything I'd hoped it to be, I wouldn't have. But it is confident, clear. It drips with charm.

My hands look for something to do, and wind up pulling both my newsie-style hat and my scarf off and mopping my very not-sweaty face with them both. I realize I'm basically hiding behind them and force my errant extremities to my side, then approach her, hat literally in hand.

"Hi," I say. "Do you mind if I talk to you?"

"Oh, I don't mind much," she says. She reaches for her tea. "I find it doesn't often help if I do."

"Oh," I say. I don't mean for my face to fall, but I can feel it doing so. I turn away, hopefully before it has a chance to ruin her day. "Sorry to bother you."

"Excuse me," she says, "but I do find I would like some company, and I suspect yours will do. Please."

I turn around.

"Are you serious?" I say.

"Too frequently. Please pull up a chair. Oh! Only, if you intend to have anything to drink, please do order it beforehand. I can't abide an empty chair at my table. Too many people in this world take it as an invitation."

"Seriously, if I'm being a bother..."

She slaps one delicate hand on the table. Most of the motion is in her wrist, so it makes a satisfying slapping sound without actually upsetting anything.

"I will tell you what is a bother!" Her wide nostrils flare and her dark eyes flash. "It is that the people in this life who are the least bother are the ones most worried about being one, while those who are the least likely to be extended an invitation are also those least likely to wait for one! Please! Get yourself something to drink and then pull a chair over. If you will not, I shall be very disappointed."

Well, if there is any prospect in this world that fills me with more streams of hot and cold running anxiety than being a bother, it is the prospect of being a disappointment. I take a moment to throw my scarf over my shoulders and replace my cap, then head into the coffee shop.

As often as I walk by this place, I have never been inside before. I wouldn't have any reason to notice it if not for her, and that made it feel like the whole place was her territory, or at least, not mine.

No one is waiting for service when I enter, so I study the board and try to find something I can order without embarrassment. I have always loved the smell of freshly roasted coffee, which I have regarded as one of nature's most insidious traps ever since the first time I actually tasted it. Tea is a bit more manageable, but I'm too aware that everyone has opinions about how it should be prepared, taken, and drunk to attempt it in public.

I settle on hot chocolate, though. Coffeehouse hot chocolate isn't quite the same as homemade on a stove, but frothy steamed milk and syrup is not dehydrated powder and microwaved water, either.

I step forward and give my best attempt at a smile.

"What can I make you?" the barista asks. She has a round, pleasant face with a sparkly stud in her nose and short, spiky hair.

"One hot chocolate, please."

She rings me up, and I pay, then she turns to start heating the milk.

"Oh!" she says, "Forgot to ask: whipped cream and sprinkles?"

The question starts a war within me. On the one hand, if I do not dress my chocolate up then anyone looking at it might suspect I am being very properly adult. On the other hand, *whipped cream and sprinkles*. Boldness or some approximation thereof has already served me well once so far today, though.

"Yes, please."

"Pardon?"

"Yes, please," I say a little louder.

A man standing very close behind me, as if drawn by my worries of projecting maturity, says in a carrying voice, "What are you, twelve years old? This is a coffee shop, not an ice cream stand. Whipped cream and sprinkles!"

"I don't actually care for coffee, thank you," I say, still in interacting-with-customer-service mode.

He's a little less than a head taller than me, compactly built but wide across the shoulders. His arms seem long to me. That's the first thing I notice on most guys: their reach. I wouldn't care to say why. He wears a blazer with patches on the elbows and a smell like bananas clings to him. I suspect the electric pipe in his breast pocket has something to do with that.

"You've probably never had *good* coffee, then," he says. "You know, coffee is a lot like chocolate: people think it needs a load of milk and sugar and other rubbish to taste good, because they've only ever had stale, over-processed garbage. Did you know the coffee 'bean' is actually a berry?"

"Is that so?" I say.

There is a smile that I have seen on the faces of other women that is both an armor against men like this and a beacon to other women. I don't know if I really know how to make it, but I give it my best shot.

"Oh, yes! And like any other fruit, it can be very sweet. This is the only coffee shop in town that serves proper coffee, which is why it's the only one I come to. When I saw you come in, I knew I'd never seen you before, which meant I knew you were in for a treat. I can't stand here and let you miss out on that."

"That's very kind," I say, "but I'm really trying to cut down on caffeine."

"Then you shouldn't order chocolate." He turns to the barista. "Carla, she'll have..."

"I'm already making her order," Carla says.

"Then she'll also have..."

"You know, I'm fine ordering for myself," I say. "I don't want coffee. I don't like coffee."

"Well, you can't stop me from ordering an extra one," he says.

"Have at it," I say.

"And you're not leaving until you try it."

"Are you going to stop me?" I say. "Physically?"

"What? I mean, I wouldn't... but you're not going to."

"Well, I'm not drinking something I don't like because you think I should, and I'm not staying here one second past when I have my drink."

"Here you go," Carla says, reaching across the counter with a steamy mug piled with whipped cream. "You know, I had a hunch and added a little splash of French vanilla, not so much that it tastes vanilla but just a hint? It's how I make it for the regulars, and I think you'll like it."

A look passes over her face for a fraction of a second. It's half apology and half concern. I understand. This guy is a regular. She has to be *nice*. She sees me, she's here. I think she'd support me if something were to happen, beyond the drama that's already unfolding, and probably nothing will.

Probably.

Most of the men who get in your way and won't listen when you say no the first time will stomp off with nothing more than a few parting insults. The problem is that the ones who will do worse don't look any different.

"That sounds lovely," I say, giving Carla a quick nod and taking the mug with both hands. "Thank you."

"Oh, so, you'll let her take liberties, but my suggestion is brushed off?" the man says.

"It's not my fault if you don't know the difference between a nice gesture and... what you're doing," I say. "And you know what? I bet if I had told Carla that I don't care for vanilla, she'd have apologized and made me a new one, not stood in my way and told me to try it anyway."

"Okay, but there's still no reason you can't try the coffee," he says.

"I don't need a reason!" I say. "Are you going to get out of my way?"

"You don't have to be so rude!" he says.

"Are you going to keep me here?"

"I shouldn't have to!"

"You don't have to!" I say. "No one's making you!"

"Hey!" Carla says. Her voice cracks when she raises it. "You have to go now."

"What?" the man says. He rounds on her, and I see the naked fury on his face. I flinch, shrink back within myself, when his arms come up. "What the fuck, Carla?"

"You are... causing a disturbance," she says. "It's upsetting people."

He looks around.

"There's no one here but me!" he says.

"Her," Carla says. "And me. Get out."

"Fine, just get me my coffee."

"GET OUT!" Carla screams.

He looks back and forth between us. The look on his face says that something very wrong has happened, that he can't quite make it add up, and then he leaves, stomping out and slamming the door.

"Sorry," I say to Carla.

"It's okay," she says.

"Are you going to be in trouble?"

"Maybe, maybe not," she says. "There have been complaints about him before. The owner says he hasn't hurt anyone, though? He's an artist."

"Yeah," I say. "Thank you. For the vanilla."

"Yeah."

We exchange another set of nods and then I head outside. The woman who makes the bees has put away her tools and out a sketchpad, and she's now bent over it, drawing anatomical sections of insects in what I think is charcoal. They look more like ants than bees.

I watch her from what I hope is a respectful distance, wondering if I've missed my window.

"I've been thinking," she says, "about branching out." She blows on the paper, then looks up at me. "Well, put that down and get yourself a chair."

I do so, and she resumes working and talking.

"I thought I heard shouting," she says. "Are you alright?"

"I... yeah," I say. "It was just a man."

"I told you about empty chairs? Well, one day a man dragged a chair over while I was working. He sat down next to me, and made sure that I knew he knew many interesting facts about entomology. I told him that I was working and he said that was okay, he didn't mind. I told him that if he distracted me, I might make a mistake. He laughed and said I was a big girl."

"That's awful," I say.

"He asked me to make him something, so I did," she says.

"What was it?"

"A yellowjacket," she says. "I told him it wouldn't sting him if he didn't make it mad, but he didn't listen. He called me an unkind name and left."

"What happened?"

"It got mad."

"Do you do this every day?" I ask her.

"The sketching?"

"Making bees."

"Weather allowing," she says. "I think I've seen you watching me before."

I lower my head.

"I don't mean to stare or anything, it's just fascinating," I say.

"It is," she agrees. "And impressive."

"Yes. Why do you do it?"

"Well, someone has to," she says. "Otherwise we're liable to run out."

"How does it work?"

"Oh, there are many aspects," she says. "Little tricks. I've learned them over the years."

"And you just let them go?"

"Bees have their own lives. That's what makes them bees. I mean, not what makes them bees in particular. But having a life is what makes my bees be bees, and not trinkets or toys."

"That's interesting, because I thought bees lived in hives."

"Everyone's got to live somewhere," she says.

"I mean, I thought they were colony creatures."

"I live in a city. I still have my life," she says. "There are solitary bees, but even in a shared hive, every bee is still its own bee. It still does what it wants."

"Isn't that just chaos?"

"What are you doing right now?"

"I... what? Nothing. I mean, I don't..."

"Are you doing what you want?"

"You mean, with my life?"

"I mean right now."

"I guess?" I say.

"Is it chaos?"

"Sometimes," I say. I'm seeing the man in the coffee shop, in my head. He had been doing what he wanted, at least as far as he could without my involvement.

"You're not running rampant, though," she says. "You're not tearing things down or burning things up. You go through life and I bet mostly what you want to do is to get along, right? You want to be comfortable. You want to feel good. You don't want to be alone."

"I guess," I say.

"And that's your nature, just as it's a bee's nature," she says. "Do you know that honeybees can control the temperature in their hives?"

"I've heard they do things like gather together and vibrate to make friction," I say. "To heat the hive. And that they can use wings for air circulation, like fans."

"Oh, yes, but it gets subtler than that. There are special bees with higher core temperatures and they can move around and regulate the temperature within themselves to change the temperature of the hive. They control how the brood develops; you know. One degree change in any direction in a developing pupa and you get a different sort of bee. Do you know how they decide, the heater bees?"

"I've always thought the queen directs the hive, somehow."

"Most people do," she says. "But there are no gears turning inside the hive, no wires running from the queen to the heaters or the workers or anyone else. Every bee, from the queen to the heaters, just does what it thinks best."

"So there's no real hive mind?"

"There is," she says. "It emerges from the behavior of the whole. Right now, what do you think the neurons in your brain are doing?"

"...firing?" I say. Neurology is not my area.

"Each neuron, how does it know to 'fire' or not?"

"I guess you'd say each one is just doing what it thinks is best," I say. "But you could say that about any cell in my body. The muscle cells in my biceps."

"Yes."

"But by that logic, the atoms that form the molecules in the cell are also just doing what they think is best," I say. "And the electrons and protons and neutrons that make up the atoms, and so on."

"Yes," she says.

"But subatomic particles and stuff, they all have to follow immutable physical laws," I say.

"Well, don't you, as well?"

"Well, yes, I can't decide to ignore the laws of physics," I say. "But I can decide to turn left or right. I can decide to take the short way home after work, or the long way that goes past the sidewalk cafe."

"I am not a particle physicist," she says, "but it is my understanding that they deal in probabilities, that the motion of particles is predictable within large groups over time rather than individual particles in the moment."

"That sounds right."

"It's true of people," she says. "A social scientist couldn't predict what you or I would do in a given situation, or even model it properly, but gather enough people together and they can begin to form predictions and determine laws. And if it's true of people, it's likely true of bees. And I daresay it's likely to be true of cells of your body."

"But if I have consciousness and I'm consciously making decisions," I say, "and those decisions determine what the neurons in my brain are doing, and the neurons are made out of atoms... there can't be consciousness in the atoms, or the neurons, can there? I mean, there's a *me* that's making decisions and everything else follows suit."

"But isn't the collective action of the neurons the same as you making the decision?" she says. "And isn't the collective motion of the particles that make up the neurons the same as their action? Or do you imagine a 'you' separate from all of those that gives the smallest particles their marching orders and it just goes up the chain from there?"

"You know, it's funny you should say that, but I dated a guy once who told me that quantum uncertainty proved free will," I say. "He said without it the universe would be deterministic, but since it existed, there was room for free will."

"I'm not sure I follow how something maybe being random is the same as it having free will. How did it even come up?"

"Well, we were talking about it in the context of, if you could rewind time and let events play out again, would you do the same thing every time?" I say. "An impossible hypothetical. I used to love talking about things like that. Anyway, I said that you'd do the same thing every time, because whatever reasons you'd had for doing it the first time would still be true."

"That seems completely sensible," she says.

"I was enjoying the conversation, but he got really mad about that," I say. "I didn't understand why. Still don't. But he shouted at me that I was saying free will didn't exist. No, actually, what he said was that I was saying *he* didn't have free will. Like it was personal? He looked at me like he wanted to hit me, then pounded the wall with his fist and stomped off."

"'Pounded the wall with his fist'," she says. "That is an interesting turn of phrase. In point of fact, he punched the wall, didn't he?"

"Well, yes," I say. "He did. Inches from my head."

"Scary," she says.

"It wasn't at the time?" Then I remember how I felt, and I shudder. "No, wait, it was. But it was also normal? I didn't see him for a day or two, and then he came back, smiling and told me that he'd figured it all out. Quantum uncertainty, he said. The randomness of electrons meant that if you rewound time and let events play out over and over again, he might do a different thing each time, and that meant he might have free will."

"Did that make sense to you?"

"No," I say.

"I think he had it backwards," she says. "If what you do is random, then you have no free will. If you're doing the same thing each time, that still leaves the possibility that you've chosen it."

"I kind of agree?" I say. "But..."

There's a scrape of metal on stone at the table behind me, at the same time as a forceful exhalation of air. I twist around and crane my neck to see a man a squat man with short arms pushing back from the table and turning his chair towards ours. He's wearing an olive drab bucket hat and a pointedly ugly gray and red sweater.

"Hold on there, ladies," the man says. "This has been an interesting enough conversation to listen to, but now you're talking nonsense."

"Excuse me," she says, "you're interrupting her."

"Someone has to!" he says. "Look, the essence of free will is *choice*, right? And if you have to do the same thing every time, that's not a choice, and that's not free. Wouldn't you agree?"

"That's an interesting point of view," she says.

"But I asked you a question. I said, wouldn't you agree?"

"You already know my thoughts on the subject," she says. "If you would like to hear more of them, you're welcome to listen."

He shakes his head, grinning.

"Darling," he says, "darling, that's just not how a conversation works. There's got to be some give and take."

"I was not having a conversation with you," she says.

"Well, it's a free country, and I have free will," he says. "And I have chosen, freely, to have a conversation with you. Are you going to respect my autonomy?"

He says this last bit triumphantly, with a gleam in his eye like he has us now. Neither of us has mentioned autonomy as a concept by name, but I have a feeling that in this moment he's winning the last argument he started with a woman about how she doled out her time and attention.

"We actually have somewhere we need to be," she says. She removes the sheet from her sketchpad and carefully puts it into a pouch, then puts the pad in another pocket. "Plans. Goodbye."

"Bullshit!" he says. He sounds personally affronted. "I've been sitting here since before she got here," he says, jabbing a finger at me, "and I know for a fact the two of you have never said a word to one another before today."

"We're old friends," I say, "and we really need to go."

"Yeah? Then you know each other's names," he says.

"Katrina," I say. It's the first thing that pops into my head. "I call her Kat, but no one else does."

"Bullshit!" he repeats.

"Her parents call her Katie, but she hates that," I say.

"And she's Anna," my Kat says, and just like that I am. "I call her Anna. Are you ready to go, Anna?"

"Yes, Kat," I say, standing up. "Ready when you are."

"Bullshit!" he screams again, getting to his feet. "Let me see your ID! If those are really your names, I'll... I'll..."

Kat leaps to her feet. She is tiny, and somehow seems tinier standing up than sitting down, but her eyes blaze.

"You'll what? You'll let us have a private conversation unblessed by your input?" she screams back at his face. "Let us leave? Let us exist in peace?"

"Don't make me the bad guy here!" he says. "I'm not the one selling a line of bullshit and getting defensive when corrected!"

"We weren't selling you anything," Kat says. "You were *listening*."

"It was a public conversation!" he says. "But shit, if you're just going to be like this about it, never fucking mind!"

He kicks the chair and storms off, his progress periodically punctuated with primal screams of "fuck" and "shit".

I watch him go to make sure that he's really gone, and then I turn back towards Kat, who is still standing. Her eyes are closed. Her head is tilted down. She is breathing forcefully but slowly in and out of her nose. Her arms are at her side, straight down, but her hands jut out perpendicular to the ground.

I'm about to ask her if she's okay when I notice behind her: a whole swarm of glittering mechanical bees, hovering in the air in two perfect formations; a pair of symmetrical angel wings formed of intricate hexagons.

She relaxes, unclenches her body and lets her hands go limp. Her eyes open. The wings break apart, the bees scattering into several separate swarms that stream away in different directions.

"That was incredible," I say, watching her watch one of them.

"I can certainly barely credit it," she says.

"Yeah, that guy was something else."

"No, he really wasn't," she says. "I was, though. I'm not usually half that brave, you know."

"No?" I say, amazed.

"Not at all," she says. "I'm snarky, which seems similar, but only from the outside."

"What made this time different?"

"I think you inspired me," she says. "You know, I've never actually balled my fists and yelled at a man like that before."

"I wasn't watching your fists," I say.

"Yes. Well. What were they doing back there, anyway?"

"Swarming," I say. "Flying in formation. They looked like wings. It was like they were protecting you, or like they were a part of you."

"That's interesting," she says.

"You didn't make them do that?" I ask.

"I don't make them do anything," she says. "I just make them.

"So they all chose to do that," I say. "Individually."

"They all chose to do that," she agrees. "But you were saying?"

"Sheesh, what was I saying?" I say. "We were talking about free will, and doing the same thing over and over again."

"You said you agree that randomness is not the same as free will," Kat says. "Do you want to know my name, by the way?"

"...is it weird if I don't?"

"Then call me Kat, because I don't think you'd ever not be Anna to me," she says. "We found those names for each other. We forged those names in fire."

"Isn't that a little melodramatic?"

"Compared to him?" she says, gesturing vaguely in the direction in which he'd departed.

"Fair point."

"I'm up now, I've put my things away," she says. "I would like to walk, Anna. Would you like to walk with me?"

"I would."

We walk, and we talk. I have so many questions in my head about the bees, but we're already enmeshed in a broader topic and not only am I afraid to come off as prying, I'm actually enjoying it.

"So, yeah," I say. "I basically agree that free will and randomness aren't the same thing. I mean, if we want to really get into it, what we perceive as random might not actually be random, and it might be the levers, so to speak, by which a disembodied conscious can affect the material world. I thought about it a lot, after that conversation, but when I brought it up again, he wasn't interested. It was like, he'd settled the matter to his satisfaction and couldn't understand why I was still interested."

"Forget about him," she says. "Do you think that explanation is likely?"

"No," I say. "I think there is something more to us than the material, if only to explain what consciousness is, but I don't believe in an external soul, and I don't think consciousness can be explained at the quantum level. I think it's an aggregate. What's the word you used? You said it emerges?"

"Yes," she says. "It emerges, it is emergent."

"Yes. I think consciousness is emergent. I think it emerges from... complexity. Intricate organizations of matter, complex chains of reactions."

"So a hive might be conscious, might have consciousness in the sense that you or I do."

"But then what about the bees?" I ask.

"What about them?"

"You say they're all acting as individuals," I say. "Are they not complex enough to have consciousness?"

"It's your theory."

"Well, I don't know where the cut-off is," I say. "But I'm pretty sure my individual neurons don't have consciousness."

"Why not?"

"Because I know that I do," I say. "Cogito ergo sum. If I know nothing else in this universe, and I probably don't, then I know that I *am*. And if I'm conscious, then my cells aren't."

"How does that follow?" she says. "You know that you have consciousness, but this doesn't mean that I don't, or a hive doesn't. Why should it have any implications for your neurons?"

"Well, you're not part of me. My neurons are. If I'm conscious, that means that what I say goes, right?"

"You're equating consciousness with free will now. Is it necessarily true that the two coexist?"

"What's the point of consciousness without it?" I ask. "If it's all just one domino knocking over the other into infinity, why is there anyone to watch it?"

"If you could set up an infinite number of dominoes, wouldn't you want someone to watch them tipping over?"

"But there's no real 'me' if I'm not deciding anything."

"I can accept that," Kat says. "But why does that mean there can't be a 'me' for each of your individual neurons?"

"Because they might decide different things than I do," I say.

"Does your body always do everything you want, exactly the way you want?"

"Oh, hell no!" I say.

"If the heaters didn't do what the hive wanted, if the workers didn't do what the hive wanted, if any appreciable number of the bees within a hive did not do what the hive wanted, the hive would die," Kat says. "Yet, they're acting as individuals. These are not contradictions."

"Then who is really making the decision, the emergent consciousness of the hive or the individual consciousnesses of the bees?"

"Why does it have to be one or the other? Why can't it be both?"

"Because... because... if the bees are making the decision, then the hive isn't, and if the hive is making the decision, then the bees aren't."

"Why, though?"

"Because either way, one of them is bound by the decision of the other," I say.

"Except that a bee can act against the hive's decision," she says. "And it's possible, albeit unlikely, that so many will do so that in practical terms, the hive is deciding against the bees' actions. But even if that never happened, if the decisions are being made at the same time, how can one be said to cause the other?"

I don't have an answer for that. After a few moments, Kat goes on.

"Think about your rewind scenario," she says. "No matter how many times a moment is replayed, you'd make the same decision. You know you would. It's still your choice in every moment, but *because* it's your choice you'd make it the same way each time, every time."

"Well, that's pessimistic," a man who had been passing by said. He looped back around and fell in beside us. He's a scrawny guy, with long, limber arms and a well-trimmed beard covering his whole face. I find my eyes drawn to the abrasions on his knuckles. I get them a lot from running my hands into the sides of doorways and walls when I'm walking. I tell myself his could be from that, too. "You don't think people would learn from their mistakes?"

"Oh, in the scenario under discussion, there's no learning involved," Kat says. "Imagine time flowing backwards, moments unraveling, until you come to the decision point once more. Everything then is as it was the first time through. You know nothing more. Nothing is different in any respect. All the factors that led you to make the decision the first time are in play exactly as before."

"What if I made the decision on a whim the first time?"

"Then that whim and everything that went into it is in your head the second time," she says.

"I think I'd figure out a way to send a message back," he says. "I'd fight to remember. I'd overcome."

"That's nice," Kat says.

"You know what your problem is? You're underestimating the human spirit."

"That's nice," she repeats.

He looks at her like she's slapped him.

"There's no need to be like that," he says, and then, mercifully, he turns back around and keeps walking.

"What was I saying?" Kat says.

"You were talking about how we'd make the same choices each time, every time," I say.

"Yes!" she says. "Only it's stronger than that: because we only experience each moment once, we only ever do make one choice. If you have two paths laid out before you, you can never choose them both..."

We're passing a row of houses with iron fences topped with fleurs-de-lis, like ornate little spears. An older man, arms long enough to reach around to the front of his mailbox, chimes in as we are almost past him.

"Your first mistake is accepting the choices life gives you as absolute," he says. "If you don't do that, you could find a way to do both, or pick a third path."

"Yes, but in practical terms, that's still making a single decision," Kat says. "Which is my point."

"You're allowing yourself to be limited by accepting the terms presented to you," the man says. "Me? I'm the master of my own destiny. That's why I'm happy with my circumstances. I chose them."

"I'm sure you are," Kat says, and I fall a tiny bit more in love with her, just enough to tip some balance in my heart that lets me know I am in love with her, and have been in love with her, and have been falling more and more ever since the moment I dared to speak to her.

We walk faster. The man falls behind.

"You can't be afraid to seize control of your life!" he calls after us.

"What I was saying," Kat says, "is that you can only ever make the choice once. This means, in practical terms, that you *can't* pick the other choices. But it's still free will, isn't it? I mean, if free will exists, it's not negated by the fact that you'll only ever pick one thing?"

"I guess not," I say. "But that one thing isn't predestined."

"Well, I've never understood people who believe that predestination and free will are incompatible," she says. "If someone could predict what you would say in a given situation with ninety-nine percent accuracy, you'd still accept that it was your choice. So why would someone being able to say it with one hundred percent accuracy change that?"

"When you put it like that, the whole thing kind of reminds me of my ex," I say.

"I'm very sorry!"

"No, I mean, the whole idea that it was more comforting for him to imagine that his actions were random than that they were fated?" I say. "Maybe that's where my objection is coming from. If we can imagine that time might be rewound, or if we can imagine a point of view from outside of time, with all my history laid out from end to end, then we can imagine a being might exist that can see from that viewpoint and know everything I ever choose, but that doesn't mean they're not still choices? It's not really that different from looking back at something that's happened and knowing it can't be changed."

"Right," she says. "So, if you can accept that free will exists irrespective of the ability to make an unpredictable choice, couldn't you accept that maybe there are multiple consciousnesses making decisions that affect you at multiple levels, and they're all acting freely?"

"I'm not sure I see the connection, except that it's two scenarios that feel like they should rule out free will," I say. "But yeah, I guess? You know what the weird thing is, though?"

"What?"

"The more we talk about this, the less I feel like free will matters as a concept," I say. "And the less I care about it."

I stop and look around.

"Are you waiting for something?" Kat asks.

"I'm kind of expecting a guy to jump out of the bushes and tell me that free will is the most important thing in the universe, that without it life is meaningless, or that by giving up on free will I'm giving in to... something. The Illuminati. I don't know."

"We could go find a more crowded street, if you'd like," she says.

"No, this is just about perfect," I say. "I'm really enjoying talking with you. I mean, I can't remember the last time I had a conversation like this."

129

"About consciousness and free will?"

"A conversation where we're just talking, not seeking anyone's approval, or performing, or whatever," I say.

"I don't have a lot of conversations in general."

"Why not?"

"I don't have a lot of patience," she says.

"I'm surprised," I say. "I think it takes a lot of patience to do what you do. I mean, with the bees."

"That's me moving at my own pace," she says. "The materials never try to race ahead of me, nor drag their feet. It doesn't take patience, just control."

"Well, it must take a lot of patience to do it in public," I say.

"That isn't patience," she says. "It's stubbornness. Do you remember the man I told you about?"

"Yes?"

"That happened the very first time I took my work to that cafe. It was a nice day, so I thought I'd work outdoors and enjoy the sun. Then that happened, and I found I had to make up my mind about whether I would let it keep me from doing so again in the future. I almost decided it wasn't worth it to try again, but I realized I hadn't actually enjoyed myself, or done the task I'd set out to do. So I went back the next day, and it was fine."

"And you kept doing it?"

"Yes," Kat says. "Every day, weather allowing. I'll sit indoors if it's not too bad to leave the house but not nice enough for al fresco, either. What might have been an occasional thing instead became a habit. Not to spite him, though."

130

"It's not for him," I say. "It's for you."

"Yes."

"So, you didn't always make your bees in public?"

"No, I started at home."

"How did you get started, anyway?"

"With cats," she says.

"Cats?"

"Yes, cats," she says. "They're larger, more like us, and in some ways, less complicated. From there I moved onto birds, which are smaller and winged. I thought for a time I would need to focus on less-social crawling insects before I could manage something gregarious and winged, but I found I really had a knack for it. It's my calling."

"You know how to make a cat?"

"Well, it's not difficult," she says. "I so hope you won't ask me to make another one. I feel guilty enough, in retrospect. We don't have anything like a shortage of cats. Bees were always the goal, for me. The cats were merely a means to get there."

"Are any of them still around? I mean, do you have any of them?"

"Oh, yes," she says. "I think I made fewer than a dozen before I was satisfied that I had the principle down. I kept three. One is my first. She's a bit scattered, but very dear. Very sweet, very shy. You put me in mind of her, actually, peering out from behind your hat and scarf like that."

"I'd love to come over and see her sometime!" I say before I can think about what I'm saying. I clap a hand over my mouth. "Oh, sorry. I didn't mean to presume..."

131

"You know, Anna, you've been very accommodating to my whims, but what I want most of all right now is to act my nature," she says.

"What do you mean?"

"As the bees do," she says. "As most things do. What did I say before? I want to be comfortable. I want to feel good. And, Anna... I really don't want to be alone."

Beryl

When bad news showed up, Beryl was always the last one to know.

Maybe it was her sunny disposition. I mean, she wasn't the perkiest person in the office. No one would call her chipper. I guess placid would be the word. Serene, untroubled. Maybe nobody wanted to tell her the bad news because nobody wanted to bring her down?

Or maybe it was less intentional than that. Maybe it was that she wasn't plugged into the same loops as everyone else. She certainly didn't seem to have much use for gossip, or to socialize with anyone outside of work. She was friendly with everyone, but friends with no one.

She wasn't naive, exactly. She wasn't uninformed. If anything, she seemed to have the company org charts memorized, and she always seemed to have time to read her company email. Even though nothing ever seemed to interrupt her workflow, she always knew the content of the latest announcements, if anyone happened to ask her.

It just didn't seem like she ever stopped to put most of it into context until someone happened to ask her about it.

For instance, when the word went around that our CFO was stepping back for personal reasons, she didn't realize that meant he was leaving. She wasn't aware that his husband had been diagnosed with cancer, though it seemed like everybody else in our work group did, and even after Sharon told her this, it was several minutes later that she came to the conclusion that this was the "personal reason".

It wasn't that you had to paint her a picture, though if you connected the dots for her she'd get there faster than she would on her own.

It was more like she was capable of knowing something with absolute certainty and perfect accuracy, of holding all the information about in her head, and yet not thinking about it in any way.

In some ways it was a remarkable talent, and it certainly helped her as a data processor. She could input more records with greater precision than anyone else in our group, maybe the whole company.

Everybody else in the team could have gone faster than we did, but we all had to stop to come up for air sometimes; take a look around.

Rest our eyes, refresh our minds.

Some of us had been doing the same or similar job for years and we knew the pace we could actually maintain was not the same as the fastest we could go. There were always trade-offs. Always. Beryl just had a gift where she could focus on the task at hand and not burn out. It was a remarkable gift, and maybe one that was wasted being a glorified transcriptionist, but I couldn't say where it might have been better applied.

In any case, it wasn't any of my business. Beryl always minded hers, and I preferred, as much as humanly possible to do the same. I think this is why I wound up in the seat next to hers, with her in the corner of the room. Everyone else who'd ever taken that seat had wound up swapping with someone else.

It wasn't that Beryl minded other people trying to talk to her. Other people would, upon occasion, mind how little she reciprocated. I didn't take it personally. I liked some of my coworkers pretty well and I didn't really dislike any of them enough for it to be worth mentioning, but my attitude was that I came into work to work, I did the work, and I went home.

We were paid a monthly bonus based on volume, so it wasn't just the idea that the company owned my time; I saw it as selling my capacity to do the work, and I wanted to get the most out of it I possibly could. I had few illusions, or at least, I liked to believe I did. I used my PTO allotment. I took my breaks. The company was going to extract whatever it could from me, so I always did my best to do the same.

In the words of the great philosopher Sally Brown, I just wanted what was coming to me. I just wanted my fair share.

I was always second in volume behind Beryl.

I had been there for three years, which was two years less than Beryl had been, and I liked the money. I didn't think the bonus structure had been designed with people who could read or type as fast as I could in mind, and I knew that ride could not last forever. The fact that Beryl had been outperforming me for two years before I ever showed up reassured me, but I knew it wouldn't be endless. Like I said, few illusions.

Even if they never re-graded the curve, eventually our whole section would become obsolete. As optical character recognition got better, the need to pay a human body to sit in a chair and type physical forms into computer forms would wane.

But while it lasted? I was going to milk it.

Our little team had grown littler still twice since I joined it. Each time management had said it was due to declining demand. I knew our company was doing more business than ever, though. It was not demand for the company's services that had declined, but demand for our labor. At this point we handled only the records that came through the scanners with garbled data and a random sampling of the ones that didn't, so our work could be compared to the computers' and the algorithms improved.

Every day, and in every way, we were building a future that had no room for us in it.

Every day, we worked our way a little further out of a job.

At a certain point, it wouldn't make sense for the company to keep a whole department staffed to do this kind of work. Eventually it would just be one person or two, and there was no guarantee I or my neighbor one seat over would be serious contenders. Not when the third or fourth best person down the line might be cheaper to keep on, and very likely have better people skills to boot.

When the third wave of layoffs hit our team, taking us from twelve down to six, I asked Beryl if she had any plans for what she would do when automation finally took our jobs.

I didn't like to interrupt her while she was working any more than I liked to be interrupted, but like I said: she was always the last one to figure out the bad stuff. I knew where we were heading and where we'd been heading. I wasn't sure she had put it together.

"What do you mean, please?" she asked.

"Each time our department shrinks, it's because they've been able to replace more of what we're doing with computers," I said, "which can do the same job better, faster, and cheaper — or fast enough and cheap enough that the occasional benefit from the human touch is no longer worth it. The computers are going to keep getting better at it. Eventually, we'll all be out of jobs."

"Automation puts people out of jobs," Beryl replied.

"Yeah," I said. "That's what it does."

"But more efficient business practices make more money."

"Which is why they do it."

"Which means they have more money to pay workers while still maintaining their profitability."

"Yeah," I said. "But no incentive. Remember: corporations are people... but humans are resources. And investors are all hung up on the idea of profit growth as like, the one overriding concern. Businesses aren't successful just because they do succeed at doing something."

"But that is the nature of success."

"Yeah, it's pretty messed up."

"This state of affairs is messed-up."

"You never thought about this before?" I asked. I had thought about it a lot over the years, especially during the layoff season. The job wasn't taxing and I didn't spend a lot of time talking, so my mind would wander.

"I never did think about this before," she said. Sometimes when we spoke, her typing would briefly slow or even pause for the briefest of instants, before resuming as quick as ever. This time, though, she was typing slower and slower, though. Was it dawning horror, or some kind of subconscious protest? "Automation costs people jobs." She stopped typing.

"Computers doing the same job as humans, but faster and more cheaply, costs people jobs. Jobs are necessary to make money. Money is necessary to buy both essential goods and services and luxury ones. This economic activity drives business."

"You got there faster than most of corporate America, if that's any consolation," I said.

Beryl said nothing, and I glanced over, and then did an honest-to-goodness double take. Beryl had just stopped. Not just stopped typing or stopped talking, but just stopped. Her fingers will still over the keyboard, right index finger stretching out towards the U key. Her mouth was slightly open. Her eyes were on the document propped up alongside her monitor, but not a muscle was moving. She was just frozen.

I wasn't even sure she was breathing.

That was ridiculous, though. *Obviously* she was breathing. She hadn't just died of shock at the revelation that businesses cared about money. She was just having a moment.

"Beryl?" I said. "Ber?"

I resisted the urge to wave my hand in front of her face, because that would have been incredibly rude, and then I did it anyway, because I didn't know what else to do. She didn't react. Not a change in her expression or posture.

"I'm sorry," I said, and I gently poked her shoulder through the sweater, and then even more gently touched the side of her face. Her skin was slightly warm and soft and felt, insofar as I actually had any kind of concrete frame of reference for what skin should feel like, normal. Nothing seemed to be wrong, except for everything.

I stifled a little shriek that I'm not even sure where it came from, scooted my chair back and jumped up. Our supervisor Judy was in her cubicle at the end of the row.

"I think Beryl... needs medical attention," I said.

"That'd be the day," she said. "Beryl's never even been sick. What's wrong?"

"I think you should see it for yourself," I said.

"You know, I hate when I'm watching Star Trek and someone tells the captain that instead of just saying what's happening," she said. "Obviously I'll come see it for myself but I want to know what I'm looking at."

"It... could be some kind of seizure?" I said. My father-in-law had a seizure disorder and sometimes had a kind of spell where he'd just go quiet and stare into space. It wasn't exactly what I'd seen in Beryl, but it was close enough that I thought it might be true. And the word "seizure" sounded urgent enough that it got Judy up and moving.

"Beryl?" she called out as she got to her feet. "Honey, are you okay?" She turned and looked at me. "She looks like she's just sitting there."

"She is just sitting there," I said, sounding in my head like Beryl herself. "Call her name again."

"Beryl? Could you come here a moment?" There was no response, and at that Judy got worried. "That's not like her. She never ignores me. Beryl? Beryl?"

The repetitions of her name became louder and more urgent, and after the second one, Judy pushed past me and hurried over to the corner where Beryl sat. The rest of the team was paying attention now, and people from the next row over were peering over the dividers. Judy put her hand on Beryl's shoulder and gave her a little shake, then I guess she tried to pull the chair out and swing it around, but Beryl's legs, slightly crooked, caught on something under the desk and she tumbled sideways out of the chair, still frozen in exactly the same position.

Judy screamed.

Helen, one of the older members of our group, quietly got done and felt Beryl's neck, and then her wrist.

"She's dead," she said quietly.

"That's not possible," Judy said, but I found myself agreeing with Helen. I couldn't explain it, but Beryl was gone. The body on the floor was just that, a body. Inanimate.

"No pulse," Helen said. "She's not breathing. Stiff as a board. I don't know how to explain it. The girl is gone."

"Call the paramedics!" someone said.

"Already on their way!" someone else replied.

"She has a medical alert bracelet," I said, suddenly coming back into myself at the mention of medical aid. "Maybe there's something we should be doing until they get here?"

"It just says not to resuscitate," Helen said, looking at it. "Poor thing. So young, she must have known she had a condition."

"A condition that does *that*?" Judy asked.

"It's none of my concern," Helen said, getting to her feet and stepping back. Everybody who did well at this job — and thus everyone who had survived the layoffs — had a certain amount of minding their own business. "Nor anyone else's.

After that, things became a bit of a blur. Management was consulted and we were sent home for the rest of the day. I didn't see the paramedics loading Beryl — Beryl's body — onto the stretcher, though I was haunted by visions of her, frozen as though she were seated at her desk and hard at work, being arranged awkwardly on it. I heard through the grapevine that there was no autopsy, because of religious reasons. I didn't know if it was true or not. I never did hear a cause of death. She didn't even have an obituary.

The thing that stuck with me was the timing, obviously. She had died while processing what I had told her. I didn't think that had killed her. I couldn't imagine a world in which that would be true. As Helen had pointed out, the DNR bracelet implied that she knew her time was short and wanted to make the most of it.

But I couldn't escape the awful coincidence of the timing, and so I never forgot my quiet but dedicated coworker.

I thought about her less as time went on, and then a lot, because the day came when the rest of us got the axe. I was kind of quietly glad that Beryl had not had to deal with that. She hadn't seem well-disposed to cope with the notion.

I also thought about her when I saw or heard the name Beryl, of course, particularly when it was used as a name for a person and not a mineral or fictional character. It wasn't an entirely unique name but it wasn't a common one. So you can imagine I jumped out of my skin when I heard her name, her full name Beryl Jones, on the news. They were talking about a local labor organizer who had just announced she was running for congress in our district as a Democrat, on an economically progressive platform. That didn't sound at all like Beryl, but again the barbed end of the coincidence hooked me right in the gut: the last conversation I'd had with my Beryl Jones had been broadly on the topic of labor and economics.

I went online and did a search for "Beryl Jones congress" and found a link to a video, bracing myself for deepening weirdness. Obviously it wasn't the Beryl I knew. Obviously it couldn't be.

But obviously I was expecting that somehow, impossibly, it would be.

I clicked the link. I opened the video. It begun to play.

It...

...was not my Beryl.

Obviously.

Of course it wasn't.

She had the same name, but she didn't have the same hair, the same skin, the same eyes or face. Her voice was different. Her mannerisms were completely different. She came off maybe a little bit too polished, but as a rookie politician maybe she'd gone through a few crash courses on presentation and still didn't have everything down pat.

Anyway, the Beryl I had known had been anything but polished, at least in her speech. Smooth, placid, but not polished.

Once I got over my initial and obviously ridiculous apprehensions, I started to listen to what Beryl Jones, labor organizer, had to say. As it turned out, it was a lot. As it also turned out, I liked what she had to say.

The video was a quick compilation of excerpts from a speech she had given, followed by her answers to some of the questions reporters asked her afterwards

"Automation is coming, whether we like it or not. Automation will transform our industries and change our way of life. We have to make the choice, here and now, to change with it. We have to make a decision about what sort of society we want to build with this and other new technologies. We have to define our values. Greater efficiency makes us wealthier as a people and more prosperous as a nation, but if this prosperity is not shared by all, it will ultimately be unsustainable."

Was she against automation? an interpolated voice asked.

"We can't stop computers from taking jobs away from people, because it does not make economic sense," she said. "Instead we should be asking, if we can free people from doing the kinds of menial jobs that computers are optimized for, what could they be doing instead? And if shifting necessary labor away from people to computers enriches a company, is the company entitled to hoard that wealth?"

Was she suggesting people should be paid for not working?

"As things stand, a company that successfully automates a process is collecting money for work it didn't do," she said. "You could ask why the company deserves this money more than anyone else who also did not do the work, especially when the labor of others allowed the company to get to that point. But moreover, I would ask everyone to think about where this leads us, if we continue to eliminate jobs without replacing them with something else. Who will be left for businesses to do business with, when no one is working?"

But surely she was not suggesting that every job could be automated.

"Never say never," Beryl Jones, candidate, replied. "That's the thing about computers. The technology never stops improving. People never stop trying to improve their programs, and now we have programs that can seek to improve themselves. We never stop learning. We never stop trying. If humanity waits until we reach some kind of tipping point, it will likely be too late. There will come a point when the rate of change is simply too great."

It wasn't exactly a solid raft of policy proposals, but I couldn't argue with her premises. Hell, they weren't that far off from my own, from the things I had said to the other Beryl Jones on that day, now several years in the past. When I thought about the things this other Beryl, the one I couldn't help but think of as the new Beryl, had said about computers getting better — which again, was not so different from what I had said — I could almost imagine this new Beryl Jones as Beryl 2.0, or 3.0, or maybe more.

A step or several up from the one I had known.

It was obviously another bizarre flight of fancy, but it made me feel better about my memories of that day, to imagine that instead of dying, Beryl had merely taken herself offline for upgrades. It not only absolved me of any possibility of having contributed to someone's death through nervous excitement, it would make me the catalyst for a journey of self-improvement.

If it were true.

Which it obviously wasn't.

It was just a thing that I could tell myself, to comfort myself.

But even knowing that, it worked.

That was the thing about the human brain, for all its illogicalness and inefficiency: sometimes the defective bits were there to cushion us. It made no logical sense but it made me feel better. Maybe when a system grew to a certain level of complexity, it needed some mysticism to it to counter the side effects no one could have anticipated for or accounted for.

From what I knew of information technology, servicing any sufficiently complicated program or system was likely to involve a certain amount of stuff that worked, but no one knew why. so maybe there wasn't that big a difference between a computerized brain and an organic one.

Anyway, I still didn't know why my Beryl Jones had died, or where this new and improved Beryl Jones had come from. I didn't know that much about any of them, though I was determined to find out as much as I could about Beryl Jones the candidate as I could, because of the one thing I did know for a fact:

If what I'd seen so far was any indication, she was definitely getting my vote. I hoped I wouldn't be alone. Computers were getting better all the time, and they wouldn't stop.

I liked to believe I had few illusions, but how could I keep going if I couldn't manage to believe that people were getting better, too?

The Numbers Game

"See, what you do is when she gives you her number, you repeat it back wrong," Scott said, speaking loudly to be heard over the pulsing, thumping beat of the club. "If she pulled it out of her ass, she won't know or care, but if it's real she'll correct you."

"How long until they catch on, though?" Matt said. "That's an easy one to get around. No. If a chick gives you her number, call it right away, in front of her. That way you know it's real."

"Unless she has a burner," Scott said.

"What kind of Feminazi harpy is so bitter about men she'd carry a burner phone just to dodge giving up the digits?"

"There's an app now. It lets them have a temporary number that works like a real one, until they don't need it anymore."

"Jesus, that's sick," Matt said. "That shit ought to be illegal."

"It's a sick world," Brodie said, bursting into their conversation and putting a big-brotherly arm around each of their necks. "And both of you losers are making the same mistake: you're giving women the chance to lie to you. Don't even make it a choice in the first place and you'll never strike out."

"Yeah, right," Matt said, wriggling out of his impromptu headlock. Brodie let go of both of them just before he succeeded. "Just walk up and tell a girl to give me her number?"

"Might work," Brodie said. "Women love assertiveness. All women respond to it, but not all respond the same. The best ones will want to test you, see how much shit you'll put up with, which is why they'll play hard to get. No, my man, the way to cut through that bullshit is simple. You do three things: one, you control the frame. Two, you don't let her know what you're after. Three, you create a scenario where you get her number, period. Just telling her to give it to you still leaves it up to chance whether she obeys or not. You have to be subtler than that."

"I thought women liked assertiveness," Scott said.

"They do! But once the hamster wheels in their heads start spinning, there's no telling where they'll stop."

"Hamster wheels?" Matt repeated.

"Dude, did you even read those links I sent you?" Brodie said. "Women are driven by emotion and instinct, but they don't like to admit this. So when there's something they need to rationalize away or justify, their brains start spinning in circles. That's the hamster wheel. It's evolutionary psychology. Because men were the providers, women never had to solve the same problems we did, so they haven't had the same evolutionary pressure towards rational thought and logic that we did."

"I guess that makes a kind of sense," Matt said.

"Damn right it does," Brodie said. "And because of feminism, women are torn between what they think they're supposed to want and what they really crave, and that sends the hamster into overdrive. Remember, their nature tells them to be submissive and follow your lead, but feminism and the matriarchal media complex keep telling them they need to be strong and independent. Is it any wonder the poor things are confused into sending off mixed signals? But with a little masculine logic, some red pill perspective, and the right techniques, you can slide past all the game playing and get what you want, any time and every time."

"Bullshit," Matt and Scott said at the same time.

"You're slick, but you're not that slick," Matt said. "You might be able to hook a 4 or a 5 or even a 6 who doesn't know it, but nothing works all the time. It's a numbers game, right? You keep going until you find the one who'll give it up instead of getting hung up on The One."

"Used to be you wouldn't have to," Scott said. "If you're a solid 7 or 8 like us, you could nail a 5 every time. She'd be flattered you were talking to her. Now feminism's taught women they deserve a perfect 10, even if they're a 4. The whole sexual economy is shot to shit now."

"Amen," Matt said.

"That's pick-up artist bullshit," Brodie said. "You two both need to get off that trip and take the red pill. It's all about an abundance mentality, bro! If you know what works, if you know how a woman's mind works, then you don't have to take the shotgun approach and hope you hit something. You can score a bull's eye, every single time."

"Bullshit," Matt said again. "It might work on some women..."

"All women," Brodie said. "Remember: AWALT."

"AWOL from what?" Matt said.

"It's more of his red pill shit, probably," Scott said.

"It's not shit," Brodie said.

"Seriously?" Scott said. "It's like something out of a movie. No, wait, it is something out of a movie."

"Yeah, I'm not taking dating advice from an obvious beta like Keanu Reeves," Matt said.

"Fuck you guys, it's a metaphor," Brodie said. "The red pill is the moment you wake up and realize all the bullshit that feminism and the female-dominated media and education systems have fed you is a pack of lies. And the red pill works, Scotty. Once you see through the veil and understand what's really going on, you can live like a king."

"Okay, so what's this AWOL thing got to do with this?" Matt asked.

"Not AWOL, AWALT. A-W-A-L-T. All Women Are Like That. All Women, dudes. They like to pretend otherwise. They want you to pretend otherwise. But they're all the same underneath that. There's science on this. Science, bros!"

"Yeah?" Matt said. "Prove it."

"Fine," Brodie said. "I will prove it, jerk-off. Pick anyone in this room and I'll walk out of here tonight with her number. Anyone. Pick a perfect 10. One of the bartenders. A female bouncer. Married. Doesn't matter. Pick any female present and I guarantee you, I will get her digits."

"Okay, maestro," Matt said, scanning the room. "How... about..."

"*Her*," Scott said, pointing to a woman sitting on the last barstool at the closest end of the bar. She wore a short black mini dress and was drinking alone. Many eyes were on her, but in the crowded club there was something like a six-foot bubble of privacy around her.

"Yeah!" Matt said. "Her, hotshot."

For a moment, Brodie was struck by the enormity of his boasts. For a moment, he was close to admitting defeat. Though he could not admit to himself a female body might exist that could not be quantified objectively on a ten-point scale, this woman was beyond perfect in ways he could not articulate.

But she was a woman, and he'd learned months ago to embrace the red pill maxim he had quoted: All Women Are Like That. The more unapproachable she seemed, the more desperate she'd be for male attention. The higher the pedestal she'd been put on by the drooling betas who slobbered over her from a distance, the faster she'd go down for a man who was willing to bring her down.

If anything, he convinced himself as he strolled over, Matt had really set him up for success.

"Oh my God, your hair is wild!" he said in a cheery, friendly tone. "You're so brave, I love it."

"Thanks," she said, without looking at him.

"I have to get a picture of it," he said.

"You don't want that," she said.

"I do!"

"I don't photograph well," she said. "I never take good pictures."

"Well, you've probably never had the right photographer. Believe me, I know how to make any woman seem attractive."

"Well, go on if you want to," she said.

"Okay, but if you're that self-conscious, maybe I should be in the picture with you. That way we can be self-conscious together."

"It's your funeral."

"Oh!" he said. "Only, my phone is old and has a shitty camera. I bet we'll get a better picture with yours."

"Okay," she said, reaching for her purse.

Some men would have already given up by this point, but Brodie had to resist the urge to pump his fist and yell yes! Every woman had an inner reservoir of objections they had to plow through before they felt comfortable saying yes. She'd stopped complaining and was now doing what he said. He wouldn't even have to fake a smile for the picture.

"Here, I've got longer arms," he said, grabbing the phone from her hand as soon as it was clear of its pouch. She offered no resistance. He positioned himself alongside her and put on his goofiest grin. The phone screen framed his face in a yellow square, but hers... wouldn't resolve into focus.

Annoyed, he tilted it at different angles and tried to vary the distance. Nothing. He kept trying, his frustration with the image's focus temporarily overriding his own ability to do so.

"Told you I don't photograph well," she said, reaching for her phone.

"No, it's fine!" Brodie said, quickly snapping a series of shots. "I'm good at Photoshop, there's a filter thing that will fix it." He stepped away from her and bent over her phone, flicking through the several pictures with exaggerated care, clucking. "I'm sure one of these will work."

"You made an attempt," she said, holding out her hand. "Give up now and you can go on with your life."

"This one's okay," he said, thumb-tapping furiously on the screen. "I'll just send this puppy to myself and..." His phone dinged in his pocket. He handed hers back. "Thanks! I'm going to treasure that."

"I'm sure you'll never forget it," she said. She turned back to the bar, but left her phone out on the counter.

Scott gave him a fist bump when he returned to their corner, but Matt scowled at him.

"You were supposed to get a number, not a selfie," he said.

"Which I texted to myself from her phone," he said, pulling his out of his pocket. He opened his messages and showed it to them. "See? That's her real number, not a burner. Plus, when I text her later, it will open this conversation and she'll see this picture as evidence of a shared experience. It's like having digits and a foot in the door. What do you say to that?"

"You, sir, are an evil genius," Matt said. "I doff my hat to you."

"Thank you, sir," Brodie said, giving a slight bow and a theatrical flourish with his hand.

Hours later, Brodie stopped at a convenience store for cigarettes on his way home. His phone chimed in his pocket. He pulled it out as he was getting out of the car and checked it.

A new text message had arrived, from the same number that had sent the pic.

It said:

"hey hmu when ur home if u want more pics"

He grinned and swiped back:

"how about now?"

The reply came back almost immediately, but its content dimmed his smile:

"when ur home"

Every woman thought she had to shit-test a man. He sighed. He wasn't about to give up control of the frame. He texted her back:

"Im home now"

Another almost immediate reply that downright pissed him off.

"lol nope"

He wasn't home, but there was no way she could know that. She was playing with him. Well, he wouldn't play back. He'd grabbed the upper hand in their first encounter and he wasn't about to give it up. She clearly thought he'd break down and beg, at which point she might give in, but she'd also be mentally moving him down several notches in her internal estimation.

The winning move here — the way to keep the frame — was to ignore her. He'd text her later, when he felt like texting her. If he felt like texting her. That "lol" was going to cost her.

He did his business with the store and then headed home. A soft light burned in the corner window of his corner apartment; the lamp he left on in his bedroom. He keyed his way inside the building and climbed the stairs to his fifth-floor apartment. He never took the elevator unless he was moving something on wheels. Maintaining frame would only take you so far with the females, after all. He needed his physique to help establish his sexual value.

He hit the light switch on the wall as he entered his living room. His phone chimed.

"how about those pics now?"

Ah. She had figured out he wasn't playing a lot sooner than he'd expected. He decided to reward her surrender with a reply:

"whatever"

He smirked. There were limits, after all, to his generosity. There had to be, or she'd decide he was too easy a mark to be worth anything.

"u like bedroom pics?"

He replied:

"sure"

A pause. A chime. A box appeared and became a picture: her, cropped at the neck. She was still wearing the dress from before, which disappointed him a little, but she was lying in bed, on a comforter that was strikingly familiar.

He smiled. This was going to be so easy.

"you know this is wild but we have the same bed set"

He sent that. The gods of the red pill were setting him up with the perfect come-on.

"lol nope"

He didn't even mind the disrespectful reply this time, because it left him in the perfect position for his follow up.

"bet you we do"

He didn't expect to be waiting long, and he wasn't disappointed.

"no"

He smirked.

"no, really we do! come over sometime and I'll show you"

Another picture came through. He saw the text before it finished loading.

"not my bed"

She'd flipped the phone out of selfie mode and taken a picture of the view down her legs and past her feet. He saw the foot of his bedframe, and past that his bookshelf and the slightly open door to the living room.

Another message jumped into view.

"come in here and I'll let you see my face my real face it doesn't photograph well but I'll let you see it with your own two eyes do you think your brain will handle it better than a camera does lol?"

He was reading it over for the third time when he heard the creaking of the bed springs and the sound of weight shifting, through the open door. An overwhelming sense of primal, superstitious dread — the misgivings he'd felt back at the bar when he first contemplated her multiplied a millionfold — and he fumbled the front door open and raced headlong down the stairs, back to the parking lot and his car.

He peeled out of the parking space and drove away into the night.

His phone had chimed once shortly after he left the apartment. He didn't check it until he stopped, outside a ten-story hotel in a town along the interstate that only seemed to exist so there would be a place along the interstate for hotels.

He'd left without a plan, with no desire in his head except to get the hell away. He'd wound up in the middle of nowhere, and only stopped because he was exhausted. The sky was still dark, but morning birds were twittering away in the trees.

The message on his phone was short and to the point:

"lol rude"

"Room 215," the hotel clerk told him when he asked for a room. "Second floor."

Exhausted as he was, he headed for the elevator. He called it, and was watching the light slowly descend from 10 when the phone chimed again. He checked it more out of habit than anything.

A picture of a door frame with the number 215 stenciled on it. Leaning against it, a familiar body in a familiar dress.

He texted back

"WTF DO U WANT????"

The reply: a picture of a hallway. At the end was an elevator.

Right after that, another shot of the hallway. The elevator doors were a lot closer. The carpet was the same as the one he stood on.

The next shot was of a hand reaching out for the down button. He glanced up. The indicator light was just hitting 3.

He turned and power-walked for the nearest exit. He could hear the bell from the door opening on the floor above as he did. He reached the door and forced his exhausted legs into a run, darting around the corner.

His phone was still in his hand, still in front of him, when it chimed and popped up with a picture: another selfie, with the head cropped. This one was taken sprawled across the hood of his car, right around the corner in the parking lot.

Panic gripped him. He texted back:

"what do you want from me"

She replied. Only text this time, not a picture. Even in the depths of his terror, he managed to feel ashamed at how relieved he was.

"i wanted nothing from u. u wanted something from me. u got it. aren't you happy?"

He replied

"NO"

She sent back:

"u got my number in ur phone u had me in ur bed u could be w/ me right now isn't this what u want? lol maybe ur confused abt what u want"

Frantically, he texted back:

"NO! I DON'T WANT THIS! LEAVE ME ALONE!"

The reply was swift as ever.

"then u leave me alone. leave us alone. delete my number. delete my pics. go home and delete your accounts, all of them. go forth & sin no more lol"

He looked at the message, looking for a threat or trick or trap. He couldn't see any. He couldn't make sense of it, but he couldn't make sense of anything.

"that's it? i do that, u leave me alone?"

She replied:

"that's it but do it or don't, idc. if u text me again, offer is off and i will see u soon <3"

158

He caught himself in the act of swiping out "fine" and stopped. He deleted the thread, then opened up his gallery to make sure the pictures deleted. He started to put his phone back in his pocket, then thought better of it. He looked around to make sure no one was looking, then he popped the back off and took out the sim card and memory card.

Picking up one of the ornamental half-bricks that was used to edge the sad little hotel garden, he smashed his phone's screen in and then hammered it repeatedly until the frame split, then threw it away.

He found himself torn between heading to the car or back up to the room. She'd been at the car last, but location didn't seem to matter to her, didn't seem to be really real for her. Plus, he was exhausted, and he'd paid for the room in advance.

On the other hand, though, she had told him to go home. Was strict adherence to that part of the deal she'd spoken of?

Maybe. Maybe not. He still had some pride, though. She — it, whatever it had been — had gotten its claws into him, gotten him scared, riled up really, but now it had moved on. He'd let it chase him out of his own home, but how could he ever maintain frame with any female if he let the fear of it chase him back home with his tail between his legs?

No, he'd taken out a room and he'd stay in it, then drive home rested and refreshed and feeling more like himself.

He was reaching for the door when a warbly but unmistakable chiming sound erupted from the trashcan near to it.

He ran all the way back to his car.

Brodie did close all his accounts. He stayed away from the club scene for a while, and all the other scenes. He left women alone. He didn't even look at them. He didn't hang out with Matt and Scott anymore, or any of his other friends, really.

He got a new phone only when it became necessary for work-related reasons, and with great reluctance. He turned off text notifications completely, so that not a sound or a pop up arrived to herald a new message.

At first he checked for new texts only when he was told to expect one, and then he started doing so every couple of days regardless, and then it became part of his daily routine.

Every day that passed and nothing happened, no texts arrived out of the blue, and no pictures, he relaxed a little bit.

It was almost a year later when started checking out women again, then months before he started cautiously feeling them out. He still panicked a little when they looked at him a certain way he couldn't quite define. He told himself he was being silly, that not all women could be like that one, but the fear was primal, the reaction deep-seated.

Still, it diminished in time.

He didn't belong to any forums any more, wasn't active on social media, but he missed the sense of community he'd had what some people called the man-o-sphere, the red pill Reddits and the MRA blogs and even the pick-up artist forums that had helped him take his baby steps in the art of constructing and maintaining frame. He started browsing them again, even if he didn't participate.

As he did, he found that the further he got from the events of that night, the easier they became to put them in their proper context. It couldn't have happened like he remembered, that was impossible. He'd been drunk, he'd been exhausted. Probably the whole thing was just the guys messing with him, anyway. They had been jealous of his prowess, of the clarity the red pill had given him, and sought to take him down a peg. Hadn't they goaded him into boasting? Hadn't they selected his target?

And it had rattled him, he was now ashamed to admit. They'd had a good laugh at him. Well, he was man enough to laugh at his own mistake, and didn't they say that he who laughed last laughed best?

Once he could laugh about it, he found his confidence returning, until finally he found himself back in a bar.

Not the same bar, not even a club, really, but a bar.

There was a girl alone at the bar. He gauged her as a 4. He smiled. This would be a nice confidence booster for both of them. He was just about to make his move when his phone chimed.

He had never turned the text notifications back on for his current phone, and he had long since forgotten what its default text sound was. He knew it wasn't what he had just heard, though, because what he had heard was the sound from his old phone. A sick, sinking certainty swept over him as he pulled it out and looked at it.

The text was from a number he had tried his best to forget. It was just five letters.

"AWALT"

He looked up at the 4 he'd been contemplating. His phone buzzed and chirped again in his hand. He looked down at it.

"All. Women."

Inside, Looking Out

"You weren't lying about the view, Nora."

The windows ran the length of my studio apartment, incorporating a sliding door out onto the balcony. We were on the wrong side of the building to watch the sunset, but the twilight sky made a nice backdrop for the city.

"After I spent so long building it up, I'm glad it meets your approval," I said. "Would you like to go outside?"

"No, thank you," Jade said. "I'm more comfortable on the inside looking out."

"You've always given me that impression. Hey, if eyes are the windows to the soul, do you think windows are a building's eyes?" I asked. She winced at the attempted witticism, but sheer awkward inertia kept me going. "Which I guess would make us the soul?"

"What... what made you say that?"

"The persistent, mistaken belief that I'm clever?" I said. Then I noticed how pale and still she'd gone. "Sorry. I guess it's a creepy idea, if you think about it."

"It's okay," she said. "I just... I have a window thing."

"I'm sorry, I thought you liked them."

"I do," she said. "That's part of the thing. Don't worry about it, though."

"Okay. Anyway, if you like the view, I'm really glad I didn't meet you last year."

"I wasn't here last year."

"I know," I said. "This is just the first place I've lived that has a view. It's also the smallest place I've been in, since college. Studio living at loft prices."

"Where do you sleep?"

"The couch, or wherever I get tired. You get used to it."

"I spent enough years couchsurfing to know I could, but also enough to know I'd rather not," she said.

"I could see that. The place does have its perks, though." I gestured upwards. "Like the high ceilings."

"And the view."

"Let it never be said I'm not a woman with views." I held up my stemless wineglass. "Can I offer you a drink?"

"Please," she said. She sank down onto the overstuffed sofa that dominated the sitting area. "Whatever you have there is fine."

"You've only been in town a year?" I asked as I offered her a wide-mouthed glass of my favorite local pinot noir. She cupped it in her hand like a snifter of brandy and made a show of slowly swirling it while sniffing with an upturned nose. I smiled. Despite the weird misstep with my joke, I thought things were going well.

"Not a year," she said. "Let's see. Six months? Six months."

I took a seat in the comfy chair opposite her. I had considered sitting next to her, but face-to-face seemed better for conversation. It wasn't like we would be shouting across a cavernous hall.

"You made friends quickly," I said. "We're generally pretty insular, a tough crowd to break into, but by the time I noticed a new face popping up, it seemed like you knew everyone."

"It's a skill I picked up late in life, believe me," she said.

"You didn't have a lot of friends growing up?" I asked, trying to sound sympathetic. I knew what that felt like. It was a common story, among queer folk.

"What a question." She shook her head, though she was smiling.

"Painful subject?"

"Not one easily explained."

"You don't have to, if you don't want to."

"Oh, I want to," Jade said. "I don't know how I can ever be close to you if you don't know. I just... I'm not sure how to make sense of it. It's not something I can just fit into a nutshell. I mean, it's really quite a story."

"We have plenty of time, but I get the feeling time isn't the only issue."

"You could say that."

"I want to know you better, Jade, but you don't owe me anything. I have a couple of movies lined up on Netflix if you don't feel like talking."

"No, I want to tell you. I'm serious about that. That's part of why I accepted your invitation. You've probably noticed I'm a little less guarded, the fewer people are around."

"I have. Though I've also noticed that you like being in a crowd."

"I like people, and I hate to be alone," she said. "But I prefer to be at the center of things, without being the center of attention, if that makes sense."

"On the inside, looking out."

"Yes. Exactly. But I thought if I was alone with you, behind closed doors, the words would just sort of tumble out of me. Now that I'm here, it's not so easy."

"Is there anything I can do to make it easier?"

She took a long, slow swallow of wine, then looked out the window again. She didn't look long. Maybe there wasn't much to see. Night was settling in behind the glass.

"Well... maybe," she said.

"Maybe?"

She looked down at the floor, then closed her eyes. I didn't prompt her again. I sipped my wine and waited for her to gather her thoughts, or her courage, or whatever it was she needed.

"I think it will be easier if you tell me something first," she said at last, then opened her eyes and lifted her face to me.

"Fair enough," I said. That sounded too grudging, I thought, when she'd been so hesitant. "I'd love for you to get to know me, too. What do you want to know? Childhood memory, family secret, political views?"

"I don't mean like a quid pro quo thing."

"Good, I prefer tit-for-tat."

She laughed, with a note of exasperation

"I'm serious, Nora!" she said. "There's just something I have to know, to be safe, I guess."

"I will tell you anything you need to know to let you know that you're safe," I said. "Ask away. I promise to take it completely seriously."

"Have you ever experienced something that you didn't feel like you could explain to anyone?"

I laughed. I couldn't help it. I felt terrible, but I honestly couldn't.

"What?" she said.

"You mean apart from liking girls?"

"Nora!"

"Sorry, I shouldn't have laughed," I said. "But I *am* serious, Jade. Even without anyone filling my head with 'the gays are of the devil'... well, I didn't have anyone telling me it was normal, either. Or possible. I just knew that things were *supposed* to be one way, but they were another way. It was like the world was upside down and only I could see it, or like I was an alien stranded among humans and I had to figure everything out for myself."

"Oh," Jade said. "I didn't think of it like that. It wasn't like that for me. At least, discovering my sexuality wasn't."

"You're one of the lucky ones."

"Don't know about that, but I had what you might call an unconventional childhood," she said. "Even apart from being queer. When I was growing up, I figured out that I liked girls pretty early on, but I never saw a relationship with another person as a possibility."

"Me, neither. Can I tell you, though, the thing that changed that for me?"

"What?"

"It was when I finally found someone I felt like I could talk to. One of my cousins, a few years older than me. She was straight, but she knew a little bit more about the world than I did. She knew that 'lesbian' wasn't just a mean word for opinionated women and girls who wouldn't put out. Learning that changed my life, maybe even saved it. Lesbians existed, they were human, and I was one of them. And you know, even before she told me that I wasn't a lonely freak, alone in the world? Even just telling her about it and realizing that she was listening and that she believed me made a lot of difference."

"Okay, I admit, you've just about sold me," she said.

"Only just about?" I waggled my eyebrows. "Well, what can I say to... *seal* the *deal*?"

"Pretty much anything but that!" she said, stifling a laugh. "You were so smooth there for just a minute, but then you lost it."

"Fear of success. I'm a self-saboteur."

She laughed this time.

"But really, Nora, it would make it easier if I could know that you'd listen and believe me. That's why I asked you that question. What I mean is, have you ever experienced something that defies all explanation, something you'd be afraid to talk about because people would think you'd hallucinated or made it up, but that you know happened? You don't have to tell me what it is, just tell me that it happened."

My first response had been glib, if heartfelt. With the obvious answer out of my system, her question was a little harder to laugh off.

Had I experienced such a thing?

Yes.

Yes, I had.

What I had experienced was not only unexplainable, it was impossible. Yet, it had happened. I knew it had. I had a box full of the impossible tucked deeply away as proof. So deeply, in fact, that I might not have thought of it, except Jade had said *a window thing*.

I shivered just thinking about it.

"I'll take that as a yes," she said.

"Yes."

"Okay," she said. "Then I'll tell you my story, and while you're listening, I want you to keep that experience, that feeling, in your head."

"It's not actually something I like to think about," I said. "I was scared out of my mind at the time. The fact that it has no explanation just makes it worse."

"I don't mean the event itself," she said. "But after. The way it felt to know something happened, know you couldn't explain it to yourself, and so you'd never in a million years get anyone to believe it happened unless they would just trust you and take it on faith. Can you do that?"

"That, I think I can do."

"Then I'll tell you my story," she said. "I've thought about telling it to someone, anyone, so many times before. I always thought that if I did, I would start something like this: the house that I grew up in was peculiar in only two regards."

"Oh, excellent beginning."

"I'll never make it through this if you give critical feedback."

"Sorry. Please continue."

"The first peculiar thing about it was the windows," she said. My skin prickled. "The second was everything else. The upper floor had no windows at all. That was where my bedroom was, along with the bathroom, and the library."

"Only one bathroom in a two-story place? Was it an older house, then?"

"I think it must have been," Jade said. "Though the layout and decor would have struck you as modern. Open floor plan for the living space. Eggshell walls and beige carpets, laminate counters and linoleum floors in the kitchen. Nothing remarkable."

"But everything was peculiar?"

"Well, for one thing, the linoleum never peeled," she said. "I think questions will only leave you more confused for now, though."

"I was just going to ask how many people were in the house."

"I'll get to that. The thing about the upper floor was that if you didn't notice the lack of windows in the bedroom, you might not have thought anything was odd about the house at all."

"I'm sorry, but you said 'the' bedroom. It... it wasn't just you, was it?"

"I thought you wanted a story, not an interview," she said.

"I'm just trying to get a proper sense of things."

"That's you all over, isn't it? You have to play detective. I think that's why you like me, you know: the mystery. I'm afraid that once you have me solved, you'll lose interest and drift away."

"A human being is not a mystery to be solved," I said.

"You're being smooth again."

"Thank you. Or sorry, as may be appropriate."

"Are you sure, though?" Jade said. "My life is made out of secrets."

"Whose isn't? That's why we're not meant to be solved. If I spent twenty years learning all of yours, you'd just have another twenty years' worth of secrets."

"They'd have to be real doozies to match the secrets of my first couple decades. Anyway, I think the only way you'll get the sense of things here is by listening. I've already told you that everything about my house was peculiar."

"Yes, you did."

"So whatever frame of reference you're using to try to glean answers in order to show how clever you are isn't actually going to apply," she said.

"I'm just trying to show you that I'm engaged with what you're saying," I said. "I want you to know that I'm listening, Jade."

"The best way to show that is by *listening*."

"Noted."

"If you began in the upstairs, as I did, your first sense that anything was odd in the house would come as you descended the staircase to the ground floor. The open plan meant that from the stairs, you could plainly see the windows in the front wall, and there were a lot of them, including a big picture one at the foot of the stairs. Only nine were actually visible from the stairs, but twenty-one total. They were all different shapes and sizes." She took a drink. "Well, that's the storied phrase, but mostly they were different rectangles, not *all* different shapes. None of them were the same size or design as any other, is what I mean. Of course, I didn't think there was anything odd about them. They were all I knew. And you have another question."

"I didn't say anything!" I said.

"I can see it on your face, waiting to pounce," she said. "Might as well not fight it. It's going to distract us both if you don't get it out, I think."

"It's just, you said that you began in the upstairs. What do you mean by that?"

"That my first clear memory was of waking up in my bedroom. I was seven years old. I don't know where the number came from, only that it was in my head and I was sure of it, as sure as I was that my name was Jade. Nothing about the house was familiar to me, but nothing about it struck me as strange, either."

"Is this story at all allegorical?"

"If it is, nobody's ever explained the meaning to me," she said. "I'm telling you what happened."

"I don't doubt you." I didn't. My own experience was too vivid in my head, bolstered by her story. "It's just that it's a very unusual story, that's all."

"That's why I have to tell it to you this way," Jade said. "As weird a story as it is, it was an even weirder childhood, but it was all I knew."

"So there were twenty-one windows on the ground floor?"

"Twenty-one along the front wall. Though, since the house didn't have a front door, or any other door, I only consider it that because it's the wall I faced when I came down the stairs. There were eleven and seven windows in the side walls, and seventeen in the back one. The kitchen had the fewest windows of any of the downstairs rooms, and that kind of skewed the count downward for the back of the house. I say 'rooms', but really, they were areas. It wasn't just the front door missing. There were no doors period, downstairs. I didn't think of it at the time, but when I compare it to other houses, I'm not sure how the bottom floor held up the upper one. There were just enough hints of walls to denote different areas. "

"This sounds pretty... imaginative."

"Look," Jade said. "I'm not going to demand that you believe me, but if you want to hear this, don't doubt me to my face, okay? I've had plenty of opportunities to doubt myself over the past decade."

"Sorry," I said. "I was just looking for a word that wasn't 'strange' or 'weird' again. I believe what you're telling me, Jade. I can't see any reason you'd have to make it up, and I don't have any reason not to believe."

"Cling to that."

"It gets stranger?"

"Be quiet and see," she said. "Anyway, there were a total of fifty-six windows in the house, all around the outside of the ground floor. None of them were alike. None of them looked out onto the same scene."

Was there some universal law that weirdness must revolve around windows?

"How did that work?" I asked, instead of saying that aloud.

"I had no idea," Jade said. "I still don't. It just did. I didn't have a television in the house, so I watched the world outside. You might have thought that would be interesting enough on its own, but I knew what a TV was, and when I found a window that looked in on one, I would watch it until someone turned it off, or I had to leave to go to the kitchen or the bathroom. The windows would change when I wasn't watching them, you see. Not always right away, but often enough that I couldn't count on coming back to find them pointing at the same scene. Other than the one ironclad rule that they never changed while I was looking at them, I never worked out a pattern behind them. I didn't care about that when I was younger, of course. I just accepted it as a thing that happened."

"That actually makes a lot of sense. As much as any of this does," I said. "I'm sorry, I'm about to ask another question. I don't want to throw you off, but I just need to make sure I'm understanding."

"Shoot."

"I was picturing these windows as if they looked out on people's yards or something, but you wouldn't find many TVs outside, facing a window."

"No," Jade said. "You wouldn't. Some of my windows looked out, some looked in. It seemed like they were about half and half, but since they would shuffle themselves when I wasn't looking, it wasn't like I could do a census."

"Were they like portals connected to actual windows?"

"I don't know if I'd use the word 'portal'. I don't think it was possible for anything but light and sound to be transmitted through them, and that was only one way. It *did* seem like everywhere my windows looked through, there was another window on the other side, of a similar size."

"What would happen if someone opened one of their windows while your window was connected to it?"

"You know, that never actually came up?" she said. "I've never thought about that, but it never happened. I don't imagine that all of the connecting windows were sealed, as some of them would have had to have been ordinary bedroom or living room windows. But no one opened any of them when I was looking through from the other side."

"That's... somehow, that's weirder than everything else," I said. "If it's true—and I'm not doubting you, I'm just trying to wrap my head around it—but if it's true, then that would mean that there was some kind of compulsion stopping people from doing it, maybe at a subliminal level, like a superstitious dread or something. Or whatever controlled the windows could somehow predict how long you would be watching and whether or not anyone would open the window in that time. Either way, there are some creepy implications about free will here."

"You really do like figuring out how things work, don't you? I never thought about any of this. It was just how my life worked."

"I have to pick at things," I said. "Sorry."

"It's okay," she said. "It's not a bad thing that I'm thinking about this stuff in new ways. Getting used to the way the world works outside the house has made the house seem unreal to me. Thinking about the, I don't know, the mechanics behind it, it makes it real again? If that makes sense."

"As much as anything does. Which isn't to say I don't believe it. The world is full of things that don't make sense, and yet are true. Can I ask another question?"

"Sure."

"If some of the windows looked in on other people's houses, you must have seen... bedrooms?"

"Yeah," she said. "And yes, to the other question after that. I was never comfortable watching it as a kid, and so I didn't. As I got older? I got curious. That's part of how I figured out that lesbians existed, and that I was one, even before I knew the word."

"I guess I understand what you meant about not seeing a relationship as a possibility."

"The vicarious nature of it all is something I felt weird about, later on. At the time, though, there was no sense that I was violating anyone's privacy. No one could know I was there. We couldn't affect each other or communicate. I was never really sure what I was seeing was *real*. I was pretty sure it was, but it was kind of like looking back in time, or into another world."

"Maybe it was?" I said. "You saw different places, why not different times?"

"I don't think so," she said. "Yeah, some showed daytime, some showed night. When it was summer in some, it would be winter in others. Eventually, when I started paying attention to the larger world through glimpses of news and things, I figured out that they were all showing me the same day, plus or minus 24 hours, but somehow the same time. I figured that out before I figured out time zones, if you can believe it."

"I guess I'd be surprised at how much you learned, period," I said.

"Oh, I learned lots of things," she said. "There was nothing to do but watch through windows and read books. When I was very young, I learned most things from the library. I didn't find classrooms very interesting to watch, though I loved seeing children my own age. When I got older, I got a lot more fascinated with the idea of formal education, though the fact that I couldn't choose when to receive any and could only get fragments of a single day's worth of lessons at a time kind of hampered my ability to educate myself. Mostly, it just gave me ideas for things to look up."

"How well was your library stocked?"

"Well, it was kind of like the windows. Every time I went in, the shelves would be different. It was a little more forgiving in that if I took a book off the shelf, that book would stay put at least until it was reshelved. That made it better for learning complex things than window-watching."

"I suppose the kitchen must have been the same as the library," I said.

"I can't tell if you're teasing me again, or trying to figure things out again."

"No, it just makes sense," I said. "I've been wondering how you ate, but didn't want to ask. No way in, no way out, food's got to come from somewhere, right? Why not a magic fridge, magic self-stocking cupboards?"

"I don't know about magic," Jade said. "But yeah. Each time I opened the fridge, it was like someone else's fridge inside. I didn't think of it that way at the time. It's only after I got out into the world and had a chance to look at other people's fridges that I realized this. Somehow, there would almost always be something that interested me in the fridge."

"That sounds like magic to me. Sorry, not trying to tease you."

"I know what you mean, though," she said. "I really wish all fridges worked like that. You don't know how many times I'll close a fridge and open it again, hoping to find something new."

"I think everybody does that, though. That's why I said it sounds like magic."

"The cupboards were more stable. Stuff would disappear before it went bad or when it ran out, and be replaced by something fresh, sometimes the same thing and sometimes different things. I'm not sure if the contents changed to reflect my tastes over the years, or if my tastes changed because the contents did. I don't know. I didn't starve, though."

"But you were cooking for yourself at seven?"

"No, I was scared of the stove until I was in the double digits," Jade said. "I don't know where that came from, I just had a very strong idea that it wasn't something for me to touch. It didn't matter, though, because there was always something ready to eat in the fridge. Somebody's leftovers, maybe. I don't know."

"That's kind of sad," I said.

"Well, I don't know if I was really eating other people's food. It might not actually have been anyone's actual fridge on the inside, you know? There's no way of knowing now."

"No, I meant... never mind."

"Tell me."

"You've been talking like you were born in the house at the age of seven with all this knowledge in your head."

"You say 'all this knowledge,' but believe me, I didn't know shit as a seven-year-old."

"You knew your name," I said. "You knew your age. You knew that the stove was not a thing to fuck around with."

"Yeah, what seven-year-old doesn't? Didn't you know that when you were a kid?"

"I did," I said. "My mother was very clear on the subject."

"I never had a mother."

"Somebody taught you better than to touch the stove," I said. "Somebody told you your name and how old you were. I don't think you learned English from windows."

"I learned snatches of more languages than I know the names of," she said. "But no, as far as I know, I've always known English."

"Do you know your first word?"

"No, do you?"

"I don't remember it," I said. "But I'm told it was 'mama'."

"I don't remember mine, either. I don't remember being born. I didn't say I was born in the house, I said my first clear memory was there. I think a lot of people don't have clear memories of their childhood, so I'm not *that* unusual."

"Sorry," I said.

"It's not a problem. I got my clothes the same way I got my food and other supplies," she continued. "Stuff would disappear from the closet or dresser when I'd outgrown it or when it fell out of my favor, and new stuff would appear as I needed it, suiting my needs and tastes. I couldn't just close the closet and wish for something, of course."

"You've tried explaining this to someone before," I guessed.

"Yeah. How did you know?"

"Because that last part was the kind of thing I want to ask," I said. "But probably not something that would have occurred to you."

"You're right."

"Who was she?"

"A girl I met, a bit after I got out," Jade said. "I was a lot freer with my explanations then, but the fact that I didn't know what was normal made it harder for me to describe what my life was like. People just thought I was weird, making things up for attention."

"How old were you?"

"Twenty-four. I had no identification, no legal history. I can't imagine what I would have done if I'd looked or sounded 'foreign' to the people in charge of figuring out what to do with me."

"No kidding. What did you do?"

"Well, I figured out pretty quickly that I looked younger than I was," she said. "People didn't believe me when I said how old I was anyway, and a homeless teenager on the cusp of adulthood raised fewer questions than a twenty-something who came out of nowhere did. So I became a teenager. If you look at my driver's license, it'll say I'm twenty-three now."

"You look a bit older than twenty-three, but not much," I said. "I can tell you had a baby face."

"Yeah."

"So... you did get out, then?"

She threw a pillow at me. Well, it was a throw pillow.

"No, I'm still trapped there to this very day!" she said. "What do you think? Anyway, the question of getting out never arose in my head. Even after I had a reason to leave, it never seemed like an option. Before that, I didn't think of myself as being trapped in the house, it was just where I lived. More than that, actually. It was my world. No matter how fascinated I was with the world outside the windows—and believe me, I was often extremely fascinated by what I saw there—it was always a little bit scary, while the house wasn't. Not at first."

"What changed?"

"When I was eleven, I broke my first window," Jade said.

"You what?"

"Not on purpose!"

"Sorry, I didn't mean to sound judgy, it just took me by surprise," I said. "But... wait, this had to be like twenty years ago, then?"

"Not quite, but yeah, close," she said. "I'd *hit it* on purpose, with my shoe, because I was mad at what I saw there. You know, I don't even remember what it was. It might have been a bird. I got really mad at birds for some reason, as a kid. I think I saw them as bullies? I don't know. It made sense to me at the time."

"Most things we do as kids do. Just out of curiosity, was this one of the rectangle windows?"

"No, it was a circle," she said. "Like a porthole on a ship, sort of. Why?"

"It made me think of something, but that's not important."

"The point is that I used to throw things at windows when there were birds on the other side of them. A rubber ball. A shoe. A book. They would always bounce off harmlessly, and so I never thought twice about doing it. Until the time I threw a shoe, and the window cracked."

"Did it not just fix itself the next time the window cycled, or whatever?"

"No. And the thing is that I'd damaged things around the house before. I'd spilled juice on the carpets, I'd chipped the edge of the kitchen counter, I'd broken a couple of bed springs, but every time I left the damage alone for a bit, it would be gone. Cleaned up. Repaired. The linoleum never peeled."

"You totally jumped on the bed as a kid, didn't you?"

"Well, I had to make my own fun," Jade said. "The point is, I somehow knew that the window was going to be different, that it would stay broken. And so I avoided it for a while. I spent a lot of time in the library, and then I avoided the corner of the house where it was. It was in the living room, and I didn't have to go through that to get to the kitchen, so I ignored it. I paid attention to other windows, putting it out of my mind completely."

"So completely you forgot to avoid it?"

"Yep. When I went back into the living room, the crack was not just still there, it was bigger. It had only gone about a quarter of the way across before, but it stretched out over the whole width. Worse, the window was *broken*."

"Didn't you just say that?"

"I mean, there was something fundamentally wrong with it," she said. "The top of the pane, the part above the crack, was bright. Indoors, but sunlit. When I got close, I could see that it was someone's kitchen. The bottom half was dark, and I thought it was just showing nothing, until I got close and saw that it wasn't blank blackness but a dark space. There was a wall opposite the window, like wet cinder blocks. I could just make them out. I could *smell* the damp through the crack, Nora. I don't know if I can explain how much the whole thing scared me, or why. The smell made it worse, because I'd never smelled anything on the other side of my windows before."

"What did you do?"

"Left for a while, then came back."

"What happened?"

"Well, the top part cycled, as you say, but the bottom stayed the same. Exactly the same. I kept trying to get it to change, but it never did. That dark space was always there. Eventually I found an M.C. Escher poster in the back of my closet, and I covered the window up and tried to forget about it."

"Which print?"

"The one with the people climbing stairs at all the angles."

"*Relativity*," I said.

"If you say so. Anyway, I'd already stopped throwing things at birds by that point, and I was *really* careful around the windows from that point on. But... accidents happen."

"You broke more windows."

"I did," she said. "I'd go months or a year or even two in between breaks, but it would always happen, sooner or later. It was almost like the first one I broke opened a seal or something. I don't know. There might have been an element of self-fulfilling prophecy, once the idea was in my head that it could happen. I'd gone four years without a single break, and then it kept happening."

"Well, I'm sure you were taller and stronger," I said. "More likely to stumble into a window, more likely to damage it. You probably had more accidents as a kid than you did as a teenager. You were just of a size where it mattered less."

"Maybe. I don't know. I guess that makes me feel a little better, thinking about it that way. The thing is, I'd be really careful right after it happened, avoid going downstairs at all except to get food and then carry that carefully back to the stairs. Then I'd start going downstairs more but giving the windows a wide berth. Sooner or later I'd be drawn back to them, and when nothing bad would happen, I'd relax, let down my guard. And then, eventually... you know."

"Accidents happen."

"Right," she said. "Some of them were just little dings, little chips. But they would always grow, go from a little dimple that would go dark the next time the window shifted to a spiderweb, and then eventually the whole thing would be cracked and the spaces between those cracks always showed the same dark place, what I thought of as the basement-place."

"Did your house have a basement?"

"Not except for the one in the broken windows, and there was no door or stairs to it, if it was connected at all. I knew what basements were, and the thought that what I was seeing might actually exist beneath my feet is another thing that made me nervous about being downstairs."

"Did you cover up all the broken ones?"

"Yeah, but that wasn't a perfect solution. Because I would look at the posters and pictures, and know what was behind them. I could avoid looking at one corner, but when I couldn't go anywhere downstairs and not have a broken window in my line of sight, covered or not, that was when I started to feel trapped."

"Even though you'd spent your whole life as you knew it in a place with no exit?"

"You have to understand, I had always felt like I was sort of in the center of things, surrounded by light and life," Jade said. "But I came to think of the dark place behind the broken windows as real, and the other images as fake. Because the basement-place was always there and it was always the same. Other places never lasted, and I knew that they were always one good hit away from showing me what was behind them."

"How many windows did you break?"

"Well, only seven, before I reached the tipping point," she said. "But that was enough to make them unavoidable. The eighth one was the big picture window in front of the stairs, in what would have been the entryway. I was coming down the stairs for a late night snack with a book in my hand when I fell, and it went flying. I can see it flying through the air in my head, though that's all imagination. I was falling down the stairs at the time, not watching the book."

"Understandable."

"Anyway, it hit dead center, and left a big, spidery crater right in the middle. I knew looking at it that there was nothing I could do to cover it up, and that even if I did, it would be the first thing I would see every day for the rest of my life when I came down the stairs, and I just couldn't take it."

"What did you do?"

"What anyone does when they're trapped," she said. "I panicked. I'd lost a shoe on my way down, a big, clunky platform thing. I picked it up, and I swung it heel-first right in the middle of the crack. If I was trying to do anything, I guess I was trying to hasten the process. I don't know. I just know that the glass exploded outwards where my shoe hit it, leaving a jagged hole surrounded by cracks. In the space between the cracks, there was the dark place. In the middle, though, in the hole? There was nothing."

"Darker darkness?"

"Nothingness," Jade said. "I mean, it was black, but I had actual darkness right next to it for comparison, and they weren't the same thing at all. So, I hit the window again, made the hole bigger. The black nothing was better than the dark something, but I wasn't thinking on that level yet. I just wanted to *destroy* the window, stop it from showing me that place. This had never seemed like an option before, and now it was. So, I took it."

"Understandable."

"I'm glad you think so. When I was done, there wasn't a bit of glass left in the pane. Just a rectangular nothingness, hanging there in the wall. All the shards of glass that fell onto the sill or into the room, I picked up and threw out into the nothingness.

They seemed to disappear as soon as they passed beyond the wall."

"Did you try reaching through it, or sticking something into it?"

"I might have eventually, if things had gone on long enough after that. Anyway, once I was finished with that window, I did the others. The broken ones. I didn't take their covers off for the first blows, so I didn't have to look at that place until it was a bunch of splintery shards. When I was done, I felt... transformed."

"It must have been very... empowering?"

"I'd say that's the word, yeah. I felt like a goddamned superhero, to tell you the truth. I'd just bashed the bogeyman in the face a hundred times. But then I started thinking. I had a solution to broken windows, but not to the problem of breaking them. There were forty-eight windows remaining. I figured out that if I could keep from breaking them any faster than one every year or so, I *might* not run out of them before I died."

"But you'd spend your entire life worrying about breaking them."

"Yes," Jade said. "They were the only resource in the house that didn't seem to be renewable. And even if I had a way to banish the basement-place once it started showing up, I would always know it was there, would always be afraid it lurked behind the remaining windows."

"So what did you do?"

"What you probably think I did."

"Broke them all?"

"Every last one. I smashed them out, one by one, and removed every single piece of glass from them."

"Didn't that strike you as short-sighted?"

"It might have," she said. "If I'd let myself think about it. I think if I had actually stopped to think about what I was doing in the middle of it, I would have come apart completely, convinced that I'd wasted so much of my most precious commodity. I might have lived out the rest of my life in that house, ruing the day I'd snapped and broken all those windows for no reason. But I finished the job, and all I felt then was satisfaction. Relief. Not an ounce of regret. I'd given up the views, but I knew it was worth it. That probably sounds weird, even granting the premises of the story leading up to it."

"Not really," I said. "It sounds like the sunk cost fallacy."

"What?"

"It's a form of cognitive dissonance. Once you have committed yourself to a course of action and can't take it back, your brain begins rationalizing it as a good thing, even if confronted with evidence that it was a net loss. So the more resources you spent—that is, the more windows you smashed—the harder it would be to consider any possibility that made your actions wasteful."

"I don't think it was a net loss, though," Jade said. "The cost of keeping the windows had become too high. Watching them had still been a thing to do—the only thing to do, apart from reading—but it hadn't given me any joy in years, and I didn't have any peace whether I was watching them or not. It's possible I would have come to fear the gaping nothingness in time, if I'd had to live with it any longer, but at the time, I didn't. I just went upstairs and went to bed."

"Let me guess: that was when the experiment ended. The next day you woke up in a hospital, or a voice on a hidden speaker spoke to you and told you it was over."

"No," she said. "Or not exactly. If it was an experiment, I think there was one final stage. The next morning I woke up to a feeling of dread. I was convinced that when I went downstairs that the windows would be back, all intact yet all showing the basement-place again. Or worse, that they would still be gone, but the comforting blackness would be replaced with that awful darkness with no glass between it and me. But I knew that wasn't the case as soon as I reached the stairs, because I could already see the picture window."

"It was back?"

"It was changed. It was now a set of three sliding panes, looking out on a grassy lawn. All the windows that were visible from the stairs were back, but different. They all opened now. Some were sash windows, some were casement windows..."

"I don't know what those are."

"Yeah, well, I've learned a lot about windows. The point is, they all *opened*. None of them had before. And none of them were screened in. I went around the house looking at them all just to make sure I knew what the deal was, but even before I reached the bottom of the stairs, I think I basically understood what was happening. I was being given a way out. My choice of fifty-six of them, in fact."

"So you packed a suitcase and picked your favorite one?"

"I didn't think that far ahead. It didn't seem worth comparing them, because who knew if they'd stay the same? I didn't even want to head back upstairs or go anywhere where I wouldn't have at least one in my line of sight, because would they even still open if I left them alone? Remember, as odd as

189

this whole thing must sound to you, my life had a rhythm and an order to it, but this was unprecedented. So I found one that looked nice, and I climbed out through it."

"Where did it lead?"

"Iowa," Jade said.

I snorted.

"What?"

"You spent, what, twenty-some years looking at the entire world and you picked *Iowa*?"

"It was less than twenty, and I didn't pick Iowa, I picked a sunny scene with trees and grass and a sandy beach beyond it," she said.

"There are sandy beaches in Iowa?"

"At least one," Jade said. "It was a vacation resort on Lake Okoboji, as I learned later."

"Sounds more like Florida to me."

"It was *Iowa*, I'm telling you," she said. "Believe me, I was still there in the winter. A groundskeeper saw me climbing out of a beach bungalow window and yelled at me, and I ran. He didn't chase me or anything. I think he thought I was a teenager sneaking out, which meant I wasn't his problem."

"And you were twenty-four?"

"Twenty-four, suddenly homeless, broke, and with no idea how to fend for myself in the outside world. The story of my next couple years is honestly the painful one. Getting put into the system as a teenager gave me a legal existence, but the cost was pretty high. Some of it's funny in retrospect. I mean, it took me a long time to get used to the idea that what I saw when I looked through a window was really there. The whole idea of going around and looking at them from the other side weirded me out for the longest time. Still does, sometimes."

"I had a cat like that, growing up," I said. "He loved looking out the windows, but he'd give me the most mortally offended looks if he ever looked down and saw me in the yard. I think it messed with his sense of place, somehow."

"That's funny."

"Anyway, you don't have to tell me about your life before you got settled, if you don't want to. I know where you came from, and I understand why that's important."

"I might tell you, someday," she said. "I almost didn't tell you about the house, but so far, I'm glad I did."

"So far?"

"Yeah. It's like you said: just telling someone helps, and you're taking it pretty well. It's just that right now, you're like a window I'm looking out of. Right now I like what I'm seeing, but I'm kind of afraid to turn away, in case you change while I'm not looking."

"You mean, you're afraid that after you leave, I'll never call you again and stop looking you for around town."

"That would be one of the kinder awful things that might happen, yes."

"Well, it won't," I said. "I'm glad you told me. And I do believe you."

"Thank you," Jade said. "It's enough that you don't disbelieve me."

"But I believe you. You asked me at the beginning if I'd ever experienced something that I can't explain. Jade, I think everyone probably has had a brush with something strange, but mine... well, maybe I should just tell you."

"You don't have to," she said. "Mine is kind of an integral part of who I am. It's why I don't talk about myself much. I know you want to get to know me, Nora, and I *want* you to know me, but there's no knowing me without knowing my past. I doubt your 'brush with strangeness' had quite as much impact on who you are, not to minimize it."

"It didn't. But Jade, I want to tell you about it anyway, not for myself, but for you. I think it'll help, in the same way that it helped me when my cousin told me that lesbians were a thing that exists."

"Okay," she said.

"Wait, maybe I should show you instead," I said. "Just sit right there."

My front closet barely got any use outside of winter, which meant it was where I shoved everything I didn't have a place for or didn't want to think about. Buried at the back of it was a battered box of corrugated cardboard, on which I'd written the words "handle with care" years before.

The contents were already broken, but they had been when I'd labeled it. I just didn't want them being handled carelessly.

The box tinkled as I pulled it out.

"It happened about five years ago," I said, putting the box down on the coffee table in front of Jade. "I was living alone, in a third-floor apartment in the cheap part of downtown. It was summer, but I kept my bedroom window closed because the fire escape was right there, and I'd always been nervous about it. I was just going to bed, not even undressed, when I heard something hit the window. I turned and looked just in time to see glass exploding inward. Well, I ran out of the room, out of the apartment, so fast I didn't even grab my phone. I called 911 from the neighbors and told them my apartment was being broken into."

"Did they take anything?"

"Jade, there was no 'they'," I said. "There wasn't even a break-in. The window was intact. I would have thought I imagined it, except the police found this."

I opened the box and tipped it towards Jade. She leaned forward, her face screwed up in curious confusion, then lit up in recognition.

"Broken glass?"

"Some of the pieces used to be bigger," I said. "But I've carried it with me through three different moves since then. A lot of it was right under the window, like it had just fallen in. Some was scattered around the room, like it had been thrown in. Some of it was tangled up with my lace curtain. The cops decided I was being punked, rather than thinking I was punking them, I think mostly because I was so freaked out by it all. But I know what I saw, and that's why I gathered it up and why I've carried it with me."

"This was... five years ago?"

"July," I said. "I'll bet July's the height of the resort season in Iowa. The date's not etched onto my brain or anything, but I could find it out pretty easily. What do you want to bet the date would mean something to you?"

"I don't know the date that I left. It took me a while to get my bearings. But it was in July... and it was five years ago."

"So, five years ago, one of the windows you broke out was looking into my bedroom. It's the part of the story that I *know* happened, because I experienced it, too, but I think it's the part I have the hardest time believing."

"It does seem improbable, doesn't it? There must be billions of windows on the planet. I could probably go my entire life without meeting anyone I ever saw through one of them, much less someone who was on the other side of one I broke."

"But what's more probable?" I said. "That there were two inexplicable window-breaking-related phenomena happening at the same time? I think it would be harder to believe they're not related."

"It actually makes me feel better, to think that they are," she said. "I used to wonder if the world outside my windows was real, but now that I'm out in it, sometimes I wonder if anything that happened to me in there was. Now I know."

"Now you know. This is it, Jade. This is your *'lesbians exist'* moment."

"You're self-sabotaging again."

"I am become Nora, Destroyer of Moments."

"I wonder, though, if I had climbed through that window that same night, while it was showing nothing but blackness, what would have happened? Would I have ended up in your room?"

"If so, you would have been arrested for breaking and entering," I said. "I wouldn't waste my time with what ifs, if I were you. You had no reason to think those darkened windows led anywhere, much less to pick mine out of all the ones you broke. The points is, you got out."

"Yeah, I did."

"Do you ever regret leaving?"

"I couldn't have stayed. It cost too much."

"What if you could have, though?" I said. "If the broken windows had just repaired themselves to begin with, if there was no dark place behind them all? Would you rather have your house with fifty-six windows and where you had everything you ever needed, or would you rather be out here in the world where you have to work and pay bills and remember to buy things, and the scary things are just as real but they aren't always on the other side of a window?"

"Well, I didn't have everything I needed," Jade said. "I didn't have other people. I didn't have love. I didn't think I'd ever have those things, but that doesn't mean I didn't *need* them. Also, I didn't have any control."

"I've never met anyone who feels like they have control of their life."

"I can see that. I mean, I used to be able to stay up as late as I wanted and sleep in whenever I wanted, and I can't do either of those things anymore, because I have two jobs to work. I can't be careless with my apartment or possessions the way I was before. But the thing is, when I say I *can't* do these things, what I mean is, I can but there will be consequences. I have that much control, Nora. I have that much choice."

"Just like you made the choice to take out the windows."

"Like I made the choice to climb out through one of them." She nodded. "Even if everything else that followed from that moment had just been me coasting, what I did that day was still more of a choice than I ever made before it, and that's got to count for something."

"Just as I thought."

"What?"

"Sunk cost fallacy," I said.

"Nora?"

"Yes, Jade?"

"Put your box of glass away before someone gets hurt."

Sometimes, There Are Dolphins

Honeymoon Island, off the gulf coast of Florida, was connected to the mainland city of Dunedin by a causeway. It was a state park, open every day from eight a.m. until sunset. The beaches of Honeymoon Island were laid with shells as other beaches are covered in sand, with a fresh batch deposited daily by the gulf water tides.

The water as seen from the shore presented a shimmering spectrum of ocean hues, from sun-dappled silver to sparkling emerald to deep azure and many incomprehensible blends in between. The near-constant wind blowing in off the gulf keeps the clouds moving at a brisk pace, ensuring that even the most overcast days often present an interesting sight when the sun begins to dip below the distant waters at the curve of the world.

None of this had made much of an impression on Clara. She'd enjoyed the first afternoon at the beach well enough, and had had enough fun splashing around in the surf and collecting shells that she hadn't minded staying to stare at the horizon with her mother.

"Sometimes, there are dolphins," her mother had said excitedly. "They skim right along the shore, swimming in a pod. They trace the causeway and follow the outline of the island. Sometimes they jump and show off, or swim back and forth. They don't always come, of course, but when they do, it's usually it right before sunset."

There hadn't been any dolphins, though, that night or any of the five that followed. Each night, her mother had repeated the words "sometimes, there are dolphins," at least once, with a little less fervor. Clara had gone from resenting her mother for dragging her out each night to feeling sorry for her.

This was the last night of their vacation, and now Clara was excited even though her mother wasn't.

It was all because of the book.

She'd found it in the crawlspace over the garage of Grandpa's old rundown little retirement cabin days ago, but it had taken her some time to learn how to read it. She'd never seen a book like it before, one not printed with orderly uniform letters but written by hand, many hands. Some of the letters were loopy and sprawling, some were spider-leg thin, but they all crowded against one another on pages that seemed like they should have been roomy enough to accommodate anyone.

Looking at the writing had given Clara a headache at first, as well as an odd, fluttery feeling in the pit of her stomach. Curiosity had brought her back to the book, though.

That, and boredom.

Florida was supposed to be fun, but this wasn't anywhere close to the right part of Florida, as far as she could tell. There was no Disney World here. There wasn't even a Universal Studios. There was a Busch Gardens, but her mother had said she wouldn't like it, even though the best description she had mustered of it was "like a zoo with rollercoasters," and Clara couldn't imagine anyone not liking that.

"Maybe next time," her mother had said, though this was supposed to be the final trip, when Grandpa's affairs were all wrapped up so the funny old house could be sold off.

Clara didn't know what her grandfather's affairs had been. She'd asked a few grown-ups what an affair was, but the answers had been amused and evasive.

So while her mother had spent most of her time meeting with people in suits and going through boxes in what she called the study, Clara's attention had kept drifting back to the book. In time she'd learned how to look at it without wincing, and then how to read it.

It helped when she realized that the parts written in red pen were newer and made more sense than the rest. In fact, they helped her make sense of the others. She learned to think of it as a teacher correcting a badly written paper, suggesting better words, easier words.

At some point, she had started to think of the teacher as her grandfather and imagined that he was giving her some kind of guidance, knowing how much she hated to feel confused. The day she saw some of the papers in his study marked with the same red ink in the same handwriting, she had realized she was right. That was when she decided to keep the book for herself. It would be her inheritance, the last gift from her long-absent grandfather. It would make up for all the missed birthdays and Christmases.

She couldn't tell her mother, of course. For some reason, her mother hadn't wanted Clara to know much about him. Probably she was still mad about all her own birthdays and things that he'd missed.

Clara had already somehow known she couldn't tell her mother about the book, but it felt good to have a reason that she could use to explain to herself why this must be so.

But even though she would keep the book for herself, she wouldn't be selfish about it.

When she'd found the ritual, she'd known that her grandfather had a gift for his daughter, too. He'd spent so much time marking it out, translating the instructions into simple terms and even drawing clear diagrams. All the words were sounded out in bright red ink. It couldn't be simpler.

The sea-king's summoning spell, the note beside the illegible title had read. That was exactly what they needed. If the lazy old dolphins wouldn't come out and play for Clara or her mother, she was sure they wouldn't ignore a summons from the sea-king himself, whoever he might be.

She hadn't fully believed that it would work, of course, when she'd tried it. It had just been something to do. She was a bit old to believe in fairy tales, after all. Not all the way.

But she'd... felt something, something rising up from deep inside and beneath her. She'd seen the candles gutter green and then sputter out. She might have imagined what she'd thought she'd felt, but she knew that candles didn't look like that when they just blew out.

And the book... the book had slammed shut and spun around in the center of the circle, just like it was riding on mama's old record player.

The spell had worked.

It had worked!

And so this night, it was Clara's turn to scan the horizon as intently as her mother had the nights before.

The dolphins were coming, she knew. They were coming. They'd heard the sea-king's summons and they would be coming. Her mother's guidebook didn't say if the dolphins would come from the left or the right... from the south or the north... so she tried to keep watch in both directions.

"Well, it's a nice enough night for our last night here," Clara's mother was saying. She laid a hand on her daughter's shoulder. "Better enjoy the view while it lasts. Look, the sun's dipping into some haze. Do you think it'll be swallowed up before we get a proper sunset?"

"I don't know, I'm watching for dolphins."

"Clara... I know I said there might be dolphins," her mother said. "But, honestly, it's best not to set your heart on it. Sometimes, there are dolphins, but it isn't something anyone can predict or control."

"Maybe," Clara said. She almost decided to tell her mother about the spell then and there, but she thought it would be better if she just let her be surprised.

The dolphins would come by sunset. She'd had that idea fixed in her head when she did the spell, and if she'd only been guessing about how the magic would work, she still had gotten the distinct impression that the message had been received and answered in the affirmative: *sunset*.

"Just don't get so fixated on looking for one thing that you miss everything else, okay?" her mother said. "My father... your grandfather... did that, he did that his whole life. He ignored everything else, everyone else, while he went off and searched for... I don't even know what. I've been looking through his files for a week now and I still don't know what he hoped to find. I just know that he died alone, half-crazed and full of regret. He missed so much of my life, Clara. He missed his own wife's last years. He missed so much..."

"Jeez, I'm just looking for dolphins, Mom!" Clara said, whirling around and pulling away from the hand on her shoulder. "Will you give it a rest? I'm not going to miss my whole life because I spent one night looking for the stupid dolphins that you wanted to see in the first place!"

"Sorry!" her mother said. "I'm sorry, I... that was probably projecting. This is the first time I've been back here since papa's funeral, and the longest I've been here since I was a little girl, and I've just... I've been feeling and thinking things that I left buried for so long. I shouldn't have pushed all that off onto you, Clara. I'm sorry."

"Sorry, Mom," Clara said. "I didn't mean to get so mad. I just... I knew you wanted to see dolphins, so I wanted to bring them to you."

"Oh, honey, you can't *bring* someone dolphins," her mother said, with what sounded like a surprisingly nervous laugh. "They're wild and free creatures, almost like people themselves. Honey, that's what makes seeing them so special, you see? They don't operate on a schedule or come when you call them. You can't control nature. Believe me, your grandfather wasted his life learning that lesson, if he ever did learn it in the end."

"Well, I don't know if he wasted it," Clara said, as she became dimly aware of a commotion among the other late-lingering beachgoers. "But..."

"What on *earth*?" her mother said, looking at a point behind her, somewhere out over the water. "What..."

Clara turned to look out to sea. Almost straight out from her, at a point on the horizon and moving on a path perpendicular to the nearest stretch of shore to her, something was moving... several things were moving, racing along the shining silver waters, leaping out of the water as they ran along.

"Dolphins?" Clara said excitedly. Behind the frantically frolicking figures, the sun *was* sinking into the sea.

"Those aren't dolphins," her mother said, then corrected herself. "Those aren't *just* dolphins."

And they weren't.

There were dolphins, yes, but fish of every size and description raced along beside and ahead of them.

"Are they feeding?" Clara guessed.

"Nah, dolphins don't hunt like that," a young woman staring out at the onrushing spectacle said. "They try to surround a school of fish and trap them against the surface of the water, they don't chase them down like lions hunting gazelles. And look, they're not trying to *catch* the fish... they're breaking ahead of them."

"What are they doing?" someone else asked. "I thought they were supposed to follow the shore."

"They're wild animals, they're not *supposed* to do anything," Clara said. "Right, Mom?"

She looked up at her mother for support, but her budding sense of satisfaction was nipped when she saw the look of pure horror on her face.

"Are they racing?" a man guessed. "Or being chased? Why are they trying to get away from the fish? Don't dolphins eat fish? I've never heard of a fish eating a dolphin."

"I don't think it's the fish that they're trying to get away from," the young man said. "What's that saying? If you and your friend are being chased by a bear, you don't have to outrun the bear..."

The nearest dolphins weren't so far from the shore now, and they showed absolutely no sign of slowing or stopping. Clara hardly noticed. Her attention, like everyone else's, was not on the dolphins but on the rising swell far behind them, behind the stragglers and the leaping schools of fish.

The sun set.

He rose.

Ia!

The Worm Crawls In

No one ever tells you that you have to get dressed for your own funeral.

...gonna...

I mean, you don't *have* to.

...get...

No one can make you.

...buried...

You could show up naked or in your laundry day clothes... or even just whatever you happened to be wearing when you died, like a doomed soul in a story... and probably nobody would say a thing.

Except most of that before the part where nobody says anything is basically true for anyone else's funeral, too.

You don't have to get dressed. You don't have to dress appropriately. You don't have to go at all. The difference is there are, or might be, consequences to the decision when you're alive. I don't know if I fear consequences now, or if it just feels like the thing to do because I grew up with the idea of consequences, or if it just feels like the thing to do because I grew up with it being the thing to do.

...and we're...

The song has been squirming its way around my head for days now, by the way. Ever since I realized what was coming. It just wormed its way into my ear, crawled inside and made itself at home.

...gonna get buried...

Not all the time but off and on.

Not quite enough to make me wonder if I'm in hell.

Not just because of the song, anyway.

...and we're...

It's the same lyrics that popped into my head at the most inappropriate times when I was alive, which is to say whenever I was going anywhere remotely chapel-like to bid farewell to anyone who was about to be buried. The first-person aspect never really applied before, but the song never cared. It would run through my head all the same, and it was all I could do to keep from grinning and humming it to myself at the worst, least opportune moments.

...gonna...

Now the whole thing applies almost disturbingly well.

...get buried...

I dress for my own funeral that I would have dressed for anyone else's. I mean, I choose the same clothes. The manner in which I get dressed is a little bit different.

I can't explain it because doing it requires me to not pay attention to what I'm doing. If I go and stand in my closet in front of where my formal clothes are hanging, I can't touch them. I can't touch any of them.

I mean, it's not like in the movies where ghosts go through walls and stuff.

My hand does not go through them. My hand simply does not touch them. My hand barely even tries.

...gonna..

It took me most of the first day to realize I wasn't touching things. It didn't occur to me. The thought never crossed my mind to reach out and touch something, or someone. Once I did realize this, I found I had a hard time even wanting to.

I could *want to* want to. I could think about how much I would like to be drinking an ice-cold Dr. Pepper from the back of the fridge. I could want the Dr. Pepper. But it was like having an extremely localized depression, an extremely focused bout of executive dysfunction, that made the entire notion of opening the fridge door, moving the stuff in front out of the way, then grabbing the can and opening it feel like something... not forbidden, just not possible.

...get...

It was like in a video game when an object is clearly rendered as part of the set dressing of the world and not a thing you can interact with. Like an apple on a teacher's desk that is part of the model of the teacher's desk. It might look like you should be able to get it. It might even look almost identical to other apples that you could get. But you could center your view on it, point the cursor at it, and yet the option to interact with it would just never come up.

...buried...

I can get a Dr. Pepper or a Pepsi from the fridge, I can hold it in my hand, but I can't drink it. Can't make the choice to drink it, can't even really want to drink it.

...get buried...

I don't actually know the rest of the song, by the way. I only know *about* how it goes, so what rings in my head in the rare moments when it progresses beyond the chorus is near gibberish like "birds will swim, fish will fly".

I know that's not right. I know those aren't the words. But they fit well enough with what I do know to stick.

Because I can't touch anything, I can't get dressed by taking clothes off the rack in the closet and put them on. If it's possible to will myself into looking different, it must be something like flexing a set of muscles I don't know I have, and even if I can find them, I assume I'll still have to master them, like when you're young and everything is new and you're still figuring out how to move one finger without closing your whole hand as a unit.

I can't touch my clothes and I can't even open a door, but I've found that if I'm not thinking about something when I'm doing it, it just sort of... happens. I suddenly notice that I'm in the room I wanted to get to, or that I have the object I wanted in my hand. Or its ghost, anyway.

I can't pull out a chair and sit down in it, but I can find myself sitting in a chair.

It's like when you're alive and you have the thought that you need to go downstairs and get yourself a drink, and you *know* that you're getting up and doing all of that, but it's not very interesting or important so you don't really remember it.

I once heard the theory that consciousness is generated by the act of creating memories, and so it has no continuous existence. That when we space out and then find ourselves in the kitchen with no memory of what we came in for, we're a brand-new being that was called into existence to deal with that moment by a brain that was operating on autopilot. That each time we go to sleep, we cease to be, and when we wake up...

Well, there really isn't any "we" to begin with. It's all an illusion.

I've never bought this because if consciousness is an illusion, then who exactly does it think it's fooling?

I could believe that our consciousnesses only *notice* things when they're being transcribed as memories, only notice them to the extent that they're being recorded, but I've always believed there is probably something to us beyond the material simply because there is something within us to notice, something that can look up and notice our surroundings, something that can be surprised that there's a Pepsi in our hand or whatever.

At this point, I'm about ninety percent sure that I was right that there's more to our existence than the material, given that I'm dead, my body is gone, and yet I'm still hanging around.

About ninety percent sure.

At first I thought that I was just alive, of course, and then I thought I might have been the last thoughts of a dying brain, but if that's the case, this has been one heck of an occurrence at Owl Creek Bridge.

I've mostly ruled out the possibility that this is a bad dream, though that doesn't stop me from hoping that I'll wake up from it. Hope springs eternal, right?

I know all the tests. I never understood the idea of pinching yourself to see if you're dreaming. I know the idea is that it's a dream so you can't feel pain, but you can dream that you feel pain. Supposedly you can't read when you're dreaming because the required part of the brain isn't active, but you can sure dream that you're looking at words and that they make sense.

You can dream anything, including the certainty that you're definitely not dreaming.

I compared this to a bad dream and said that I hope I wake up, but the truth is it's not that bad.

It's not that anything.

...and...

It just is.

...we're...

I just am.

...gonna...

I died, and somehow I *am*. I *still* am.

...get...

I don't think I'm a ghost, exactly.

At one point I thought that perhaps I'm the thing that makes people think ghosts exist, but I think the thing that makes people believe in ghosts is people. We'd believe in ghosts even if there was nothing more to us than matter, nothing more that follows after death except for the part where the worms crawl in and the worms crawl out.

...buried...

I died and I'm still here. Something is here. At least, I think it's here. My great fear is that I'm not the thoughts of a dying brain but the thoughts of a dead mind, an immaterial consciousness disconnected from material existence and unmoored from reality... that in the absence of any more input ever from the senses of a physical brain and body, I'm just seeing and hearing what I expect to see and hear, and I'll do that forever, my perceptions gradually getting weirder and less comprehensible as errors creep in and become the thing I expect to see.

...gonna get buried...

No one can see me. No one can hear me. If my existence is an illusion then I'm only fooling myself.

After the first time I found myself sitting in a chair that was no longer pushed in, the thought occurred to me that if the chair were really out of position because of something I did, I could maybe communicate with somebody. I could make my presence known, make my presence felt. I had the thought and I didn't know what to do with it. There wasn't any immediate impetus to act on it.

After I didn't try it, I came up with a bunch of reasons why it made sense not to. Moving things around on someone who was grieving would probably feel a bit like gaslighting someone, especially when I couldn't seem to manage it quickly enough or reliably enough to actually convey a message. I don't imagine I could cause a glass to levitate across the kitchen in front of someone or anything like that. It's easier for me to zone out and find myself having done something when nobody else is around. Other people are too interesting, really the only interesting thing in my life... my existence... right now. Maybe if I were engaged in a conversation I could absent-mindedly pour myself a glass of milk and not realize I had done it, but there's basically zero chance I could pull that off when the whole point was to make the movement happen.

I'm not even sure I'm even moving things. I don't see double when I look at a dining room chair pulled out from the table or anything, but I've changed my clothes a few times and no one has stumbled over the castoffs, which would *definitely* provoke a reaction. Once I put something down, I never see it again from the moment it's out of my sight. I noticed this at one point and then, having noticed it, I didn't feel any inclination to test it or probe the limits of it. I note this fact very dispassionately. I also note how weird it is to not feel any particular way about it, but I also don't feel any kind of way about the weirdness. It's just a fact.

I wonder in a sort of vague, disconnected way if I would feel more freaked out by all of this if my life hadn't been full of stretches where it was hard to feel anything, hard to do anything. Being dead isn't exactly like being depressed, but it's similar.

Early on I had the thought that feelings were an artifact of the physical body and that was why I couldn't feel anything. My immaterial consciousness just didn't have the juice, in the same way that my physical form had occasionally lacked what it needed to feel things properly. It wasn't long after this that I discovered I can still feel things, some things, and I can feel them quite acutely. I don't feel lonely in general, but I can and do feel lonely without you.

I don't feel sad that my life is over, but I am devastated whenever I stop and think that our life is.

...gonna get buried...

I was all alone in the world and then you wormed your way into my life, my head, my heart. You got inside me and you stayed, like a song that won't leave.

...gonna get buried...

You haunted me.

...gonna get buried...

This is why I have to go to the funeral. I don't know what's going to happen after, I don't know how long this state of existence will persist, but I haven't seen you since the car crash and I can't shake the feeling that it might be my last chance.

You haven't been by the house.

I sort of can't blame you. I don't remember how I wound up here, I just barely remember thinking I should go home and then I was. I don't know what arrangements are being made but I'm afraid you'll move on and I'll have no idea where you might go from here, or how I might get there.

I'm reasonably confident I can make it to the funeral, both because it's my funeral and that seems right, and because I'm so sure it's the thing to do that I know I can do it without thinking about it, but I don't know how I'd get anywhere else. I haven't been able to dream myself to Disney World or absent-mindedly find myself in that cozy inn on the banks of the Potomac or even get anywhere in town beyond our own neighborhood.

But I know I can get to the funeral, just as sure as I know that you'll be there.

...and we're...

How could you not?

...gonna...

How could you miss it?

...get buried...

There are things I don't think about, things I seemingly can't think about, in whatever you want to call this state of existence.

Things I just don't have any interest in thinking about. Like I'm choosing from a menu and it's just not an option. Thoughts that I suppose don't apply.

...and...

And then there's the thing, the one thing, the big thing, that I can think but which I don't want to.

...and...

And no, I don't mean the song, I mean the fear.

...and we're...

The big fear.

The only fear I've felt since before I died.

It's not that I'm going to be like this forever and it's not the thought that I might fade away to nothing or wink out like a light when some arbitrary threshold is crossed. I have thought about those possibilities and many more, including the idea that I might move on, transmigrate to some other state of existence. I can think about those things and feel nothing. I can weigh their apparent merits but I can't care about them.

...gonna...

The thing that scares me, the only thing that scares me, is the possibility that I'll never see you again.

...get...

That I'll go to the funeral and you won't be there after all.

...buried...

I'll walk down the aisle and see the coffins, our coffins, our bodies, side by side. I'll be able to see your face, altered by the accident, by your absence, by the undertaker's touch. I'll see your body, your red suit that Rhonda came over and picked out for you, laid out in the coffin, but I won't see you.

...and...

That's my fear: that your body will be there but you won't, and I'll have no idea how to find out where you are or how to get there. That if I fade away into nothing, it will be without you. That if I wink out like a light, it will be without having seen you one last time, told you how I feel. Told you that I feel. That if I should be here forever, I could roam as far as I can roam aimlessly forever and never find you. That if I should move off into the great unknown, I'll be facing it alone, knowing that I'm being carried farther and farther away from you.

...we're...

I don't know how to face that. I don't know how to face any of that.

...gonna get buried...

But I don't know how I could stay away, because it's not like I'm going to get another shot at it. In my life I often took the path of least resistance, and did whatever I could to put off an unpleasant revelation. In this case that means going, because staying means accepting that I'm alone here.

Maybe I'm doomed. Maybe it's pointless. Maybe the outcome I dread is inevitable. If whatever space I move through now were peopled with the dead I would be tripping over them, so I can't help thinking that it's naive to expect you to be there, to expect you to be anywhere.

But hope springs eternal, right? That's the absurd thing about it. It doesn't require evidence, it doesn't require thought, it doesn't require certainty or likelihood or even really possibility.

...and...

So I get dressed, or at least, I find that I got dressed.

...we're...

I let the house be back in order, for whatever that matters. Whatever that means. It just feels right.

...gonna get buried...

I let myself take comfort in the feeling that, whatever happens, whatever I find, whatever I feel... it seems like I'm not coming back here. Like I'm finished. Moving on. Whatever happens next, it's not going to be what has been happening.

It could be worse.

...and we're...

But it might not be.

...going to...

See you soon. I hope.

Hello

I guess I didn't question that she was dressed as a flapper.

It was a jazz bar, and it was Halloween.

She was hardly the only one.

At first, I hardly noticed that she was a flapper at all. It was the curl of smoke in the corner of the room that caught my eye and brought it down to her. Smoking in a bar? It was rude, it was illegal, it was unhealthy... but none of that was what was going through my mind when I saw her, the cigarette holder dangling in her fingers as she slowly let a stream of smoke escape her lips. Escape? Nothing escaped her.

She expelled it.

Slowly, but forcefully.

Deliberately. Languorously.

Dangerously.

A dangerous curl of smoke.

I noticed she was flapper because the cigarette holder fit the aesthetic, but even that was a distant sort of knowing. Everything about her from the red A-line dress to the little beaded lace headdress just fit. There were other women there in flapper costumes, but she didn't look like she was in costume at all. She was practically naked; her truest self, dressed in everything around her, the bar and the jazz and the night and all of us.

I was staring. She noticed me staring, and then I was hooked. Nothing escaped her. She reeled me in. I made my way towards her across the crowded room and it was like there was no one else there. The dance floor might as well have been empty. I felt weirdly light, like my feet weren't touching the ground.

"Hello," she said.

"Hello." I wanted to say something suave, something smooth, something... maybe a little sexy. I wanted to say *"Mind if I sit here?"* or *"Is this seat taken?"* but what came out of my mouth was, "Mind if I'm taken?"

"Not at all," she said, one eyebrow barely flicking upward. "I'd say I appreciate the challenge, but I'm not sure you'd give me one."

"Oh! I just meant... can I join you?" I said. I held out my hand to show my ring. "I am, though. Taken. Married, happily. And straight. Sorry."

If she was listening, she gave no sign. She'd taken my hand, and kissed it. Well, I say kissed, but she more sort of nuzzled it with her nose and lips around the back of my hand, then left a trail of soft kisses down between my ring and middle finger. Eyes turned up at me, not blinking or breaking contact, she proceeded to kiss directly in the spot between where the two fingers joined my hand, long, slow, and deeply. Could you deeply kiss a hand? She could. Then, eyes flashing, she bit softly on the stone of my ring and began worrying it down off my finger, as though it were a garter and she were pulling a garter off with her teeth.

"Hey!" I said, way too slow off the mark for it to matter. She got it off the end of my finger, sucked it into her mouth, and spit it out into the crowd. "HEY! I need that!"

"That's a matter of opinion," she said. "Tell you what, honey? Why don't you see if it turns up at the end of the night. If it doesn't, maybe that's a sign."

"Are you serious right now? That's my wedding ring!"

"Yeah, till death do you part," she said. "Are you serious? Because I can't help but notice you're still here."

"Well... I'd get crushed like a bug if I looked for it now," I said. "I don't really have a choice but to wait for the crowd to thin out or check if it's turned in at the end of the night, do I?"

"You still have a choice of how you spend the hours until then," she said. "I'm still holding your hand. I'd let go if you told me to, you know."

"Would you?"

"There's only one way to find out."

"What's that?"

"Tell me."

"How should I know?" I said.

"No," she said. "Tell me."

"Tell you what?"

"To let go of your hand."

"Oh!" I said. "Oh. Um... would you please let go of my hand?"

"Sure," she said, relaxing her grip and pulling her fingers away. "If you ask me that nicely, I might just hold it again."

"Look who's all concerned about consent suddenly," I said.

"You going to sit or just stand there?"

"Oh!" I said, taking the seat beside her. She edged away as I sat down on the rounded couch. I half expected – maybe hoped – that she would scoot back towards me once I was ensconced in the booth with her, but she lounged luxuriantly at the other end, across the table from me.

"So, kitten," she said. "Is this your usual haunt?"

"Not hardly," I said. She laughed at that. I couldn't see anything mean in it, but there was something mocking about it. Maybe it was just her. "I'm not really a fan of dark corners in dark bars."

"Used to be darker," she said. She pointed towards the front, where the glare of the streetlamps streamed in through the glass. "Those streetlights just went up last year. They put them up just for you, so I hope you appreciate them."

"Sure they did." I laughed. "And I don't like bars with live music, or late at night. It's the crowds. I guess... I guess I've been here once before?"

"I'd guess so."

"I don't remember having a particularly good time," I said. It had been Brad's idea of a romantic evening, not mine. I'd tried to enjoy it, but my anxiety... he'd suggested I drink to calm my nerves, and then he drank, because my anxiety made him irritable. "I'm really not sure why I came back."

"No one ever is, in my experience."

"And I don't know why I came back here on this of all nights. I think this is my first Halloween out in... basically ever."

"Well, they say you always remember your first," she said. "I'm not sure I do, to be honest. There were a lot between then and now."

"You're trying to make me blush," I said.

"I ain't trying that hard, kitten."

"I told you I'm taken," I said.

"You asked me if I mind," she said.

"That was a slip of the tongue," I said.

"Well, one good slip deserves another."

"I don't even like girls," I said.

"Well, honey, I ain't the Brooklyn Dodgers. So, do you mean to tell me you don't like me?"

"I don't know what I like!" I said. "I mean, I don't know what I mean! I mean... you've got me all confused."

"Life had you confused," she said. "Maybe I'm here to help you move on. You keep rubbing your hand, where I... you know. Tell me you're not thinking about it. About my lips. On you. Against your skin. My tongue."

"I am now," I said. "Because you put the idea in my head."

"Yeah? And what's that idea doing up in there? Something nice?"

"Flirt with me all you like, the attention is flattering, but that's all," I said. "I'm a married woman, married to a man..."

"Yeah? Where's he?"

That stopped me short. Where was Brad? I was at the bar alone. I didn't go to bars alone.

I was at this one alone, though. The last time I'd been at this one – first and last time, until now – had been our anniversary, back in June. That had been such a shitshow of an evening, I could hardly remember how it had even ended. My last clear memory of it was waiting at the curb for Brad to bring the car around.

After that, it all just kind of ran together.

It was just life, I guess.

That had been our last night out together, and now here I was out and alone.

"It doesn't matter," I said, with an air of definiteness that I hoped came through in my voice, and even more hoped would take root in my mind. "I didn't come here looking for a good time."

"Well, it's just your bad luck to wind up at a party, then," she said. "Worse luck that you ran across me. Look, I'm not looking for a relationship. We're just two souls out on all souls' night."

"Technically it's all saints' night," I said. "November 1st is all saints' day. The second is all souls' day."

"I get the feeling your mouth gets the best of you a lot, kitten," she said. "Wouldn't you rather it was my mouth doing that?"

"That doesn't even make sense," I said.

"And yet you know exactly what I mean. Funny, isn't it?"

"I'm not going home with you."

"Where even is home? This bar might as well be home. Why not here?"

"If you think I'd have my first lesbian experience in a bathroom bar..."

"I see that you're open to the idea," she said. "Now we're negotiating particulars."

"You don't even know my name!"

"Because I didn't ask," she said. "Do I look like I give a flying fuck in a windstorm what your name is?"

"What exactly are you proposing?" I asked.

"Proposing?" she said. "I told you, kitten, it's not that serious. Here's what I picture. You and me, right here. Well, you there. Me, under the table. You don't have to do anything but sit there and look pretty. You can try not to scream if you want, but it won't help."

"Here?" I said. "In front of everybody?"

"In front of who?" she said. "Trust me, no one will notice."

"While I'm screaming my head off? Writhing? Thrashing? Clawing at the edge of the table?"

"I can see you're getting into the spirit of it, so to speak," she said. "I appreciate your confidence, but trust me, no one will notice."

"We'll be arrested!"

"I might have been," she said. "Or committed. You? You'd have been asked to leave. Barred, maybe. You don't know how good you could have had it, kitten, when you had it. If you'd had it."

"Had what?"

"A life!"

"My life didn't end the day I got married," I said.

"Not the same year, anyway," she said. "Here's what I'm going to do. I'm not going to do anything you don't want, but I can tell you're not ready to say it. So I'm just going to slip-slide down under the table, very slowly, like this." She began slinking down in her seat, angling her narrow body under the large table, as she spoke. "And then I'm going to crawl slowly across, giving you all the time in the world to tell me to stop, or to get up and walk away, walk out of this joint and into whatever's waiting for you next. If that's what you want to do. If not..."

It would have been the easiest thing in the world to walk away. It should have been. I shouldn't have had to even think about it. I couldn't think, but I shouldn't have needed to. This was a no-brainer, which was convenient because I didn't seem to have a brain. In that moment, I wasn't even sure that I had a body. I felt weightless, floaty, oddly dilute. Like I wasn't really there. Like I wasn't really anywhere.

Nothing felt real.

Not the table in front of me, not the bench at my back, not the bar around us or the crowd.

Not even me.

Maybe especially me.

"My name's Liv, by the way," she said from under the table. "Still don't care about yours, but if you don't want to scream wordlessly the whole time, you might find that useful."

"Oh, you are so full of yourself," I said.

"That's going to make two of us," Liv said.

"It isn't the least bit attractive."

"Good thing for me you've got lousy taste," she said. Then she put her hands on my knees and that was real, very real. She was real, and where she touched me, I was real, too.

She didn't pull my underwear down. She didn't even really bother with them at all. She just pressed her face against it, nuzzling me through the fabric. It... it was amazing. I wanted her skin against my skin, her lips on my... lips, but I also didn't want anything to change anything about what was happening. She pressed her mouth against them, she rubbed up and down, burying her nose in the fabric, she put her lips to the front panel of my panties and she sucked, sucked hard enough that I felt it through the satin, and that was... it was... it was everything.

I couldn't keep track of everything that happened after that. The sensations were too strong, too numerous, conflicting and cascading and bleeding into one another. At some point my panties got twisted up and sort of pushed to the side, her face bearing down hard and me bucking and writhing to meet her. Without even thinking, I put my hand on the back of her head, more for something to hold onto than anything else, but she batted it away. Not knowing what else to do with my hands, I put them in the air, my hands clenching into tiny little fists. My toes were curling in my shoes... in my shoe. I'd kicked one off at some point.

If it had been over quickly I probably wouldn't have thought anything about it, but as it went on I found myself floating on a haze of pure physical emotion, looking out across the crowded floor of the bar. Hot humiliation flooded my feverish face, the feeling of excitement commingled with embarrassment adding an interesting frisson to... everything. It wasn't pleasant, but it was fun. Did that make sense? Nothing did. Everything did. I felt like I was on the cusp of understanding something, of understanding everything. I felt like something was on the tip of my tongue, a big something, a great and secret something.

I felt like I was on the cusp of remembering something I'd forgotten, something important.

Like when I walked into the kitchen and the memory of what I'd gone there for vanished as soon as I crossed over the threshold, and I knew it was something important, and I felt like I could almost remember it but not quite, but I was close, I was close, I was so fucking close... tip of my tongue, tip of my tongue, tip of my tongue...

I had never felt this way, not any of the times with Brad, not with anyone before Brad. I felt alive for the first time in... in... in...

I was screaming. Inside and out, body and voice. Spirit. Soul. All of me. Coming. Screaming. Was the bar silent, or could I only hear myself? I gave myself over to it. Gave up. Gave in. Over and over again. I came over and over again, screaming, "Liv, Liv, Liv, Liv!"

I didn't even know when she finished, exactly. I was still riding the wave of sensation, still rocking and reeling, when she slid back up into the booth right next to me, pressed up against me the way I'd expected – hoped – she would be after I first sat down.

"Next Halloween?" she said.

"Is that all you can say?"

"What more do you want?" she said. "My poor tongue's all worn out and you want me making speeches? Have mercy, kitten."

"I'm still going to be married next Halloween," I said.

"Till death," she repeated. "Next Halloween?"

"Do I have to wait that long?"

"Trust me, kitten, it will feel like no time passed at all," she said.

"Do you want to know my name?"

"Did I fucking ask for it?" She lit another cigarette. "The difference between you and me is that I know how to ask for what I want. And if you do hang around, you're going to find that out for sure."

"I've got nowhere else to be," I said.

"Not until midnight, anyway."

"Last call's at two," I said.

"Not for us, it's not," she said. "Stick around, for me, because I really don't have anywhere to be. Not anywhere I want to go. A good girl like you could go places, but believe me, I wouldn't be caught dead anywhere but here. And it gets lonely, haunting a joint like that. You wouldn't think so, but it does. I get lonely."

"You could be nicer to me, if you want me to stay," I said.

"Is that what you want?"

"Well... I said it, didn't I?"

"No," she said. "You didn't say you wanted me to treat you nicer. You said I *could*. Do you want that?"

"...no."

"Just for that, I am going to be nicer unless you say 'I like the way you treat me, Liv.'"

"I... I like the way you treat me, Liv."

"Then I'll see you next Halloween?"

"...I'll have to see what Brad says," I said. "I have to talk to him about this. I can't just... you know."

"Look, kitten, I'm here for a good time, not a... well, I'm here for a long time, too," she said. "But I told you it's not that serious. When you do see him, and you will, eventually, you can tell him anything you need to, because I'll just fade into the background. You'll have places to go and people to go there with, but I'll still be here. I will *always* be here."

"The way you keep talking..." I said. Things were starting to click into place. "I get it. You're a ghost."

"Oh, you get there eventually," she said.

"I mean, it's a cool concept but I think it might have worked better somewhere you would have stood out more. Not that you... I mean, there's a dozen other flappers here and a lot of 20s theming in general that makes it hard to tell you're being anachronistic? Plus, you didn't make it easy. I mean, you put more effort into the outfit than most, but there's nothing about it that says you're dead. It's all character work. If you really want to sell the idea, you could have put some fake blood on or some of that glowing face paint... though I guess I'm glad you didn't do that one. It might have been hard for me to explain later," I said. "I shouldn't critique your costume, though. I didn't even wear one. This is just my basic look." I gestured down at what I was wearing, and realized it was wearing a dress. "Well, my going-out look." It was my lacy white cocktail dress. "Well, my fancy occasion going-out look." I snorted with a sudden realization: I'd bought this dress for my anniversary dinner, before I knew where we were going. "Actually, I think this is the same outfit I wore the last time I was here. It's funny... I remember... I remember thinking what a shame it was to ruin it, and then thinking that was a strange thing to worry about."

"Do you remember how it got ruined?"

"Well, obviously it didn't," I said. "I'm wearing it. I honestly don't know why I thought that. I think I must have been pretty close to falling down drunk by the end of the night, though. Maybe I thought I spilled something on it? Maybe I stumbled... it can't have been that bad, though. Anyway, I'm not sure why I would have dragged it out for tonight. I guess I felt like dressing up for Halloween but I didn't have a costume? Maybe I'll dig something up for next year."

"You won't," she said. "You'll be exactly the same, ring on your finger and everything."

"You're not the boss of me," I said.

"Not until you beg me to be, with that attitude," she said. "But I guess that means I'll see you next year?"

"I guess so," I said.

"Do you feel that? It's almost midnight," she said. I didn't know how she knew, but as soon as she said, I knew it, too. It was like a change coming over the room, a charge in the air. I felt the beginnings of a pull almost as insistent as hers had been. "Time's almost up, kitten. Kiss me."

"What, like it's New Year's?" I said. "Should we do a countdown?"

"No time," she said. "Kiss me or don't, but if you don't do it fast you'll lose your chance to find out what you taste like on my lips."

"I... uh..."

"No? Then I'll kiss you. Here's your countdown, kitten," she said. "Ten seconds."

She pushed her lips against mine, and I tried to focus on it, but my attention was divided between her and the time. Midnight was coming, and I would swear I could feel it coming closer, feel the seconds slipping away. All the sound went out of the world, for the second time in one night I lost track of everything, so caught up in the moment, in those final moments, that I was left sitting there with my eyes closed when she slipped away.

I opened my eyes and found that the bar had emptied while I'd been preoccupied. The party had ended in a hurry, it seemed. The staff must have been in the back. The lights were dimmed, the music gone.

I didn't care. I couldn't care, couldn't care about anything, hold onto anything. It was like I was slipping away with the stroke of midnight, too.

I didn't really remember much of anything after that, but the one thing that stayed with me, the one thing that kept me there, was the solid certainty that I would be back for next Halloween, that I would see Liv again.

Somehow, I knew that even after I knew nothing else.

About The Author

Alexandra Erin is an author, poet, and commentator from Maryland by way of Nebraska. A pioneer in the field of internet self-publishing, she has supported herself and her work through crowdfunding since before there was a word for it, to say nothing of specialized tools. You can find out what she's working on now by going to alexandraerin.com, or follow her on Twitter @alexandraerin.

On the eve of the US presidential election is 2016, she found herself on Twitter, drinking heavily and explaining what was happening. Things kept happening, and she kept explaining, and drinking. This is now her primary vocation.

You Remember This Story

The first time you remember reading the story, it happens when you find it on the website of the hot new speculative fiction zine all your friends have been talking about. You remember it as soon as you see the title, recalling a vivid memory of sitting at the little desk in your old apartment and reading it in plain text off a BBS archive.

The desk had not been a computer desk but a writing desk, old and nice but not very ergonomic or practical for a keyboard. The awkward strain of using it left an indelible stamp on each memory associated with it, marking a particular time period in your early to mid-20s where recollections of your online activities are easiest to date.

You remember having gotten the link from a friend in one of your old Yahoo! chatrooms, remember having been told that it was hard to describe but that it was "very you" somehow. You remember this being said with an apologetic coda to it, in case you somehow took that the wrong way.

You remember thinking "What the fuck?" as you started reading, and then, "No, but seriously, what the actual fuck?" and then "HOLY SHIT. HOLY FUCKING SHIT!" and then, eventually, reluctantly, admitting that your friend was right to send it to you.

As you sit there thinking about that time, you remember how strangely familiar it all was at the time, and now you are remembering for the first time having read the story before that, in a hard-bound volume of science fiction stories in the school library when you were just in seventh grade. You remember thinking how weird it was, and how out of place. You hadn't understood it, hadn't understood how it made you feel. None of the other stories in the book had featured such raw, visceral emotion, or such bloody imagery, or what you later realized were sexual themes.

The part where the woman walks up the mountain, shedding her garments as she goes, walking on bare, bloody feet and leaving a red path up the little goat trail... you remember that part. You remember thinking back on it at random moments and trying to recall how it fit into the larger story, which exists more as disconnected images in your head than a plot. The woman, clad in moonlight. Her blood gleaming on the rocks. The knife, making its first careful incision, skin-deep and no deeper.

The deeper cuts came later.

You remember them.

Vividly.

You wonder at the zine taking a decades-old reprint, one that circulated on the internet before it was properly an internet, but it must be the same story that you know because you know you recognize the name of the author, E.M. Warfield. You click on the link and you start to read and there it is, just as you remember it.

More than you remember, even.

The story opens in a little house on a dark plain, and a family eating dinner. The conversation is so trite and banal that even though you didn't remember any of it, you remember now that the second time you read it, you thought it was no wonder you didn't remember it. You find yourself only half-reading it this time, skimming and even skipping ahead until the first mention of the woman walking up the mountain, which you now remember is intercut with the conversation of the people at the dinner table.

You are a little surprised to realize that the people are not a family, or at least not explicitly identified as such. You remembered them that way, perhaps because you made an assumption the first time you read it, or because you added that detail when you later recalled it.

They all seem to be adult, and they all seem to be quite pleased with themselves.

It's a little off-putting, really. You just want to know more about the woman. Who is she? Where is she going?

Why is she going there?

She is walking across the desert. It's not a mountain she's walking to, but a mesa, a great big sandstone bluff. You thought you had remembered her taking off her boots, but she is barefoot at the first mention of her. You go back and forth within the text a few times to make sure of that, because you had such a vivid impression in your mind of the image of her pulling off her boots without breaking stride.

Her feet are already tender and sore at the first mention, and it specifies that she has been walking for hours. It does not say from where, only that the mesa is before her. You have the impression that whatever it is the men are talking about (and you notice now that they are all men, something you don't remember noticing before) seems to be about her, though they don't appear to mention her. They speak of responsibility and accountability, and the greater good, but also opportunity, "tremendous opportunity", and they assure each other that the doubters and naysayers will be placated in the morning.

It's not a path up a mountain but a switchback trail that ping-pongs back and forth up the least-steep side of the mesa. Her feet bleed, and not just her feet but her arms and sides where she brushes against jagged edges, stumbling up the path in the dark. In your head the woman has always walked proudly, defiantly upright. It's hard to shake that image even as you read about her tripping and falling, swaying, bumping into the walls.

There comes a point in the story where the men in the house say goodnight to one another and most of them leave, while those who remain go to bed. It is not a moment weighted with importance in your memory or in the story, and it does not seem to correspond to anything significant in the woman's journey. Sometime after that, a fox appears and begins to follow after her, but it is hard to say if that is meant to be related to events in the house, or how.

The fox's arrival is followed by a pair of snakes, who slither after her, their sinuous courses always taking them over the twin bloody trails left by her feet. Before long they are slick with blood and turn the broken, irregular tracks into two curvy lines.

The procession is joined by insects: crickets and locusts and moths, and then night birds begin circling overhead, landing on the mesa in great numbers. All of them are there when the woman crests the top of the bluff, pulling herself up the last few feet because it is too steep to walk.

Already there is a great beast, a beast like a goat with the wings of a lion. That's what it says. That's what the story says. A beast like a goat with the wings of a lion. You didn't remember that, but that's what it says. The beast regards her quite calmly, and she is calm, and you are calm, too, as she goes to it, stops before it, picks up the knife stuck point-first in the stony ground before it.

It is a knife, stuck in the ground. You remembered it being a dagger, stuck in a stone. In your head it was not a natural stone but one that had been shaped and placed there, to hold the dagger, which is a knife. When you realize that the word "dagger" is not used at all in the story, the image in your head changes slightly. You see something less ornate, less elegant, more utilitarian.

She picks up the knife and turns her back to the beast, looking up at the starry sky. She feels hands on her shoulders. You remember them belonging to the beast, but as you read the story now, you see there is no mention of whose hands they are. They are simply hands, falling on her shoulders from behind. She closes her eyes, and the hands move downward, finding her hips, pulling her backwards.

You remember being confused by this, confused and a little... excited? Afraid? Both at once? You don't remember having realized it was sexual when you read it the first time, but you remember knowing it when you started it the second. You don't remember at what point the penny dropped.

It's less explicit than you remember, or imagined. Somehow, it's all less exciting. The sexual part is just not that interesting to you now. The last time you read it, you didn't exactly remember how the story ended, but the more intimate bit had left more of an impression on your young mind. This time you're waiting for the final scene, for the cuts, the careful, awful cuts, and then the peeling, the endless peeling, the stripping away, then standing glistening and exposed in the moonlight.

Then, it happens, and it's so much shorter than you remember, and the story is over and you're not sure what it was about it the last time that imbued it with such a sense of import and meaning. You were never sure before what it meant, only that it meant, and in your younger years that was enough. You realize you've been reading the story hoping that you would understand that nebulous, numinous something you had felt before, and not only have you not understood it, you haven't even felt it.

You read the author's bio at the bottom, which tells you that E.M. Warfield is an author of speculative fiction and this is their first published story. It doesn't mention if it was published before, that it was published before. You search the name and the title and they both just lead you back here. You try to remember the name of the collection of short stories it was in, but you can't find that, either.

Your best guess leads you to a book whose cover looks familiar but not only is this story not in it, it's a collection of science fiction stories set in the near future, with a theme of emerging technologies. The time period of this story is not specified, and there is nothing in it that speaks of a future, near or otherwise, nor of technologies, emerging or otherwise.

But you remember it. You remember reading it, remember having read it.

You remember this story.

You ask a few of your friends who have been talking about the zine if they'd ever seen any of the stories in it before, and none of them had. You don't mention the specific story or your memories, because you're afraid of... well, you're afraid of how it would sound, but more than that, more than being afraid of anything in particular you're just plain afraid, and you don't know why, or of what.

You never finish reading the zine. You never read any of the future issues of it, though you do read a poem or story occasionally when someone links you to it specifically.

You didn't decide to not read it. You're just not reading it, and you don't ever think about why.

You do think about the story often, then less often, though intensely when you do, and then one day, you stop thinking about it at all.

The next time you remember reading the story is when you find it in a new collection of The Year's Very Best Science Fiction Stories. You remember it as soon as you see the title in the table of contents; E.M. Warfield is not one of the luminaries among luminaries who get to be listed on the cover. When you see the story listed, you remember how weird it was finding it in the zine, a few years back, and you again remember having read it on the BBS archive, and in the seventh grade.

You also remember now the time you found it on a forum post somewhere, collecting a weird story that had been published across a series of apparently unrelated comments on different, apparently unrelated Reddit posts. The comments and the account that left them had been deleted by the time you saw it, and you remember that some of the commenters thought the whole thing was a bit of fabricated creepypasta, an internet folktale, that the comments had never existed.

Multiple people attested to having seen them when they were made, some offering screenshots, but you alone had been there insisting that it was a real story, one that had been previously published, that you'd read it in a book in junior high. The consensus at the time had been that you were making that part up to give yourself importance because the story, while weirdly compelling in its own way, was an unpublishable mess, and wouldn't have been in a public school library.

You remember now how, as you searched the invisible corners of your memory for facts that might have proven you right, you had recalled that before you even checked out the library book, you heard the story as it was told by the weird, soft-spoken kid, the younger brother of a friend of yours who, through vagaries of birthdays and deadlines had ended up in the same grade as both of you.

He was the one who would always tell you the plot of episodes of Simpsons and Seinfeld you had both seen and then ask you to explain them to him, and he had told you about this story, told you this story, describing the sequence of events in his own broad stroke fashion, and you had thought he had to be telling it wrong, so you'd gone to read it for yourself, and found that while the story wasn't just what he had described, the parts he had described were just as he'd described them.

You remember all of this as you stare at a collection of fiction from the previous year. There is a note that the story previously appeared in another collection of short fiction first published last year.

You Google it and learn that not only is the collection out of print, but the publishing house that put it out has gone out of business.

You read the story, or you try to read it. Your own recollection gets in the way. It's not like reading a story again. It's a bit like having deja vu, a bit like hearing your own voice reverberating back at you as you're trying to speak. The parts with the boastful, arrogant men congratulating themselves and each other are almost impossible to read, but even harder to skip past. You cling to them, scrabble at them like the woman scrambling her way up the side of the mesa, bouncing and stumbling and skittering along. You see her as you read about them, you feel the pain of her progress as you scrabble and attempt to find purchase on the scenes in the house and a place to stand within the structure of the story.

Her journey is intercut with their conversation, but you see them both happening at the same time. You remember her as you read about them. You remember them as you read about her. You remember this story.

The woman. The mesa. The animals and insects. The moonlight. The beast. The knife. The ruined temple. The knife. The man... no, it never says that it's a man. It never says that it's the beast but it never says that it's a man. The one who takes her from behind.

The knife.

The moonlight.

The ending.

The ending is just as unsatisfying as before. It's worse. It doesn't just fail to satisfy; it unsatisfies. It robs you of any sense of composure, of finality, of resolution. You feel the woman, standing wet and gleaming in the moonlight, bloodier and more naked than the day she was born. There's a feeling at the end of the story. Triumph? Despair?

Is she dead, or is she free?

Is there a difference?

Now you remember when you were in college and this story was in a collection of short stories in a lit class. It was one (along with Arthur C. Clarke's "The Star") that your professor had told you would be a tough sell if you chose it to write about, because he hadn't believed that genre fiction had any worth.

You remember having been first excited to realize you knew this story — you remembered this story — and then having despaired at writing a paper on it that would have changed the professor's mind once you were thoroughly reacquainted with it. You knew it was better than he believed it to be, that it was more than he knew, but you didn't feel up to the task of explaining it to him, so instead you'd written about "The Star" and been given a B, which he told you was partly for chutzpah.

You don't finish the collection of last year's science fiction. You don't even read any of it, other than the story you flipped to. You had remembered writing about "The Star" after basically being dared to, but you hadn't thought about passing on the other story. You hadn't remembered that until you started reading it again.

It's weird to you, that you didn't think of that the last time you read the story. You remembered the story, but you didn't remember that.

You shudder, and hug yourself a little, and tell yourself that memory is weird sometimes.

Years pass. You're something of a writer now yourself, or you mean to be. You want to be. You certainly write some, some of the time. You go to conventions. You do workshops. You join groups. You go to conventions.

You vote for awards.

You've just received the voter packet for the Hugo Awards. It's been a busy year, and not entirely a good one, so you haven't paid much attention to the hullabaloo around them. It sounded like some of the nasty politics of recent years has died down, and though you hate to admit it, that alone made you pay less attention to it, maybe.

So the first time you know that this story is among the nominees for best short story is when you see it in the packet, and you remember reading it. You remember reading it in the Best Of collection, you remember reading it in the spec fic zine, you remember the forum post and the BBS archive and the collection in high school and you also remember when you heard it recorded for that dark fantasy podcast a year or so ago.

You remember being a child, just starting on chapter books, and finding a battered paperback book in the pocket on the side of your mother's chair.

You remember having believed that your chapter books were the same as the grown-up books she read, and you remember having been excited to test that theory, excited and then confused, and then... excited? Afraid? Both? You remember how the ending had fascinated you, the final image, the woman standing unbowed, undone. You remember that battered paperback had been illustrated in simple pen and ink, and you realize this is where some of the images in your head that aren't in the text have come from.

There's no ruined temple in the text, but it was there on the page. The boots were from a picture, too. The woman standing upright, even while the text described her more labored passage up the trail.

The beast's head had loomed over the woman's shoulder as the hands fell on her.

That was in the illustrations.

And on the final page, taking up a full half of the dry, yellowing paper, had been an illustration of her standing, one foot higher than the other on a rock, her face a death mask framed by wavy hair, half of her body flayed and stripped to bone and viscera, with one perfect breast exposed, and that image stayed with you, it haunted you, you can remember staying awake late at nights thinking about that, that image burned into the back of your brain until you forgot where it had come from, and remaining until it was buried under the weight of other memories.

You remember this story. You remember another paperback, the cover missing and pages falling out, that was passed around summer camp. Most of the stories in it were less weird but more explicit, and most of the other campers were more interested in them, but this was the story that had consumed you, both because you remembered having read it before and had been excited to find it again, but also because you had only just sort of learned what sex was and so were just starting to grasp that the story was sexual, just starting to make sense of the things that had confused you about it before.

Some of the things.

The anthology it was in last year is out of print, but desperate to find some proof of the story's prior existence, you scour the internet until you find a used copy for sale. You find it, finally, for the price of $179.01. It's less than a year old, but it's apparently in high demand for a book that couldn't save its publisher. Maybe the nomination caused a run on already scarce used copies.

Fuck it.

You buy it anyway.

You don't know how many times you've read this story, not really, but you can't remember having read it in two different places without having forgotten it in-between. You're a little bit afraid of what it might mean, what might happen, if you can break the sequence, but you need to know that you're not... not making things up. You know?

Conflating.

Confabulating.

Memory is weird, you tell yourself, but you're having a hard time believing it can be this weird.

While you wait for the book to arrive — you paid for rush shipping — you scour the net for what you know you will find of any Hugo-nominated stories, and that's other people's thoughts.

It turns out there aren't many. Oh, many people have written about this story, but they don't have much to say about it. It seems to be a middle-of-the-road contender, is the consensus. Neither the worst short on the ballot nor the best. You find some critics who are willing to talk about the imagery being esoteric or confusing, but no one who will talk about what it means, or how it made them feel.

No one mentions having read it before. No one mentions any controversy about its eligibility due to, for instance, having been first published decades before.

But...

You remember this story.

You're waiting at home the day the book arrives, having tracked the package obsessively and called in sick to work to be there to receive it. You don't have sick time and you can't afford this, but you feel in a very real sense like you couldn't afford to miss the delivery.

The whole time it was in transit, you were waiting for the tracking to return an exception, to tell you the package was lost or damaged en route and could not be delivered, and then when the day arrived without any mishaps along the way you were seized by a powerful fear that it would be stolen from your porch, so you took the time off and were there to take it out of the delivery person's hands.

You tear the padded envelope open and start rifling through the book, until you find the story, and you start reading it, and it is just as you remember it. You realize as you read that you hadn't even really read it all way through when it showed up in the Hugo packet. The flood of memories had overcome you, sent you searching through the halls of your memory and the tubes of the internet, leading to the moment when this book arrived in your hands. You're reading it now, re-reading the same droning conversations and retracing the same steps up the side of the mesa, up to the plateau and to beast and the knife and the temple that isn't in the text.

This version has the illustrations, and they are just as you remember them, only the lines are sharper and cleaner. It's like the same drawings were done in digital ink, but they are the drawings you remember, and as you look at them you remember how your grandfather had given you a paperback book adapting classic science fiction stories into comic books for your birthday one year. That had been your first exposure to Anne McCaffrey, with a story about a boy with a broken leg waking up late for a dragon hatching, and your first Asimov, with a story about a robot who played the piano too well and yet without meaning.

You remember this story had been in it, too, with artwork that was clearly inspired by the original illustrations. The whole thing was far more sexually charged and violent than anything else in the book, geared as it was towards young readers. You remember having thought that your grandfather would never have given you the book if he'd looked at that story, that your parents never would have let you keep it, so you read it once, quickly and carefully, and then hid it away and forgot about it.

You remember it now, remember how it spent a whole page drawing the walk across the desert, even though that's covered by a few lines of text. You remember how that made the march to the mesa seem much longer in your head the next time you read it, and every time thereafter.

You remember how it rendered the fox and the snakes and the insects and the birds much more prominently. In the text they are not mentioned much after they appear, save the snakes, who cease to be a part of the story after it describes how they become slick with blood.

In the graphic novel adaptation, though, they are depicted alongside the woman each step of her journey after their appearance. They are with her atop the bluff and are rendered in a panoramic view behind her in the triumphant final panel, where she stands doubly naked and revealed.

You remember that panel and you remember how it changed the whole tone of the ending, that the woman was not alone and not just attended by the beast and perhaps an unseen lover.

The actual illustrations are much sparser, but your eyes catch on them when they appear on the page, and you lose your place, and read certain passages over, which feels like it changes the meaning. You feel the weariness of the woman as she climbs the path, but you know she is not resigned. She is driven by a certainty and a sense of triumph. You feel that her climb represents her victory, her victory over those small men in the big house, so very far away. You know that while she is the one climbing to the heavens, this is a story about their hubris and their comeuppance.

You remember your friend's little brother telling you this, and you remember your professor who hated genre fiction explaining that the theme is an inversion of the tower of Babel and likening it to an inverted Tarot card, the lightning-struck tower. You remember your mother finding you with her old pulp fiction book and telling you it's a story about how you must be careful how you treat others. You remember the librarian finding you puzzling over it and telling you that it's a story for older children, but one that everyone should read, at some point, eventually.

You remember your wife giving you a copy of this story the day that she goes into the hospice. You don't remember the marriage, or meeting her, because those things haven't happened yet. You remember before that having read it on your phone while you waited in the little room for someone to come out and tell you how the procedure had gone.

You remember reading it before going on the writer's retreat where you would write first draft of your breakthrough story. You don't remember what that story will be, though you remember that you will have been thinking about the flayed woman standing victorious beneath the moonlight.

You remember that you read it just before you broke up with him. You remember how in that moment, his voice sounded in your head like all the reedy, wheedling, whiny men who were sure of their favor and fortune. You remember having caught a glimpse of your own face reflected in the window of your car right before you climbed into it and drove away, and you remember thinking you looked like her, glistening and naked and perfect and powerful, so powerful.

It was the first time you looked at yourself and really saw a woman, and though you didn't remember that moment until now, you have never since then thought you looked half as fierce or as feminine as when you glimpsed yourself reflected in a dark window.

You remember finding the story again in your own twilight years, like re-discovering an old friend, and you remember that when you read it for the last time, you finally understood what it was really about, what everyone had been trying to tell you. What it had been trying to tell you.

You don't remember what that is, though.

Not now.

Not when you're reading the collection that you bought off the internet for $179.01, remembering all the other times you have read or will read the story.

When you finish, you put the book back in the envelope. You take it to the post office and you send it back to the address it came from, at your own expense, with tracking. You remember you should probably give the seller positive feedback, but by the time you get home, their account has been deleted.

You watch the tracking for the package. You see when it is declared undeliverable — no such person at that address. The envelope is damaged on its way back to you. It arrives, chewed open at one end by a sorting machine.

Empty.

You are not surprised.

It's not that you expected it to happen this way, so much as you remembered it.

This is not the last time you remember the story.

It's just all the times you have remembered it so far.

Acknowledgments

No one does it alone, in books least of all.

Thank you to Amanda for helping bring to life my cover out of my very rough idea, to Jack for helping spot the little things I couldn't, and to Dr. Sunny for looking at the physical design and pronouncing it good.

Thank you to my patrons over the years who have paid for these stories, and my backers on Kickstarter who paid for this book.

And thank you to my mother, who kept me safe.

Made in the USA
Middletown, DE
18 May 2019